the **atonement** series

BROKEN VESSEL

BOOK ONE

STELLA JACKSON

SYNCTERFACE™
Syncterface Media
London
www.syncterfacemedia.com

BROKEN VESSEL
ISBN: 978-0-9933860-2-2
Copyright © January 2017
Stella Jackson
All Rights Reserved

Published in the United Kingdom by

Syncterface Media
London
www.syncterfacemedia.com
info@syncterfacemedia.com

Cover Design:
Syncterface Media, London

This book is printed on acid-free paper

*To the emotionally, physically, mentally and sexually abused
without a voice:*

*The harrowing pain you feel may take time to heal
but never give up,
There will be a lifting*

Acknowledgements

Lucinda,…
This book may not have gone to print if not for you. After reading the initial script, you said, "Mum, this is fantastic! I hope you realise that this is a best seller." Thank you for taking the time to do the first edit. I appreciate you so much.

My siblings,…
For your encouragement, your love and for always being there. Thank you.

My husband, Goddy…
For constantly interjecting with inspiring suggestions; for all those hours you put up with me when I was literally burning the midnight oil. God bless you for understanding and for your words of wisdom.

Korede,…
We have always been close but discussing my manuscript with you brought us together in a way I never envisaged. Thank you so much for setting me up with the perfect publisher. I am so grateful.

Syncterface Media,…
Akin, thank you for merging your thoughts with mine to elucidate the various emotions and for making this novel a reality. Thank you for the beautiful things you said along the way, encouraging me to 'soar' in my writing. Thank you for making my publishing experience an enjoyable one. I hope and pray that this will be the beginning of a blessed and rewarding journey.

My Heavenly Father,…

Above all, the greatest thanks and honour go to You, who not only gave me the dream but provided the entire outline and plot for this heart-rending story. I have come to realise that the gift of writing comes from You and You alone.

I pray that You will use this book to touch the hearts and minds of all those who read it and may it bring about the desired response regarding the laws that govern all kinds of abuse. Thank You.

Foreword

To say that I enjoyed reading this story is simply an understatement. Captivated from the very first paragraph, every turned leaf left me wanting more. I was drawn in as a co-traveller with little Leah, whose recent stance can only be described as "Enough is Enough!" and by the end of chapter two, I had tears in my eyes, as I could see a life riddled with injustice looking for a way to break free.

As much as I tried, I couldn't put this book down. Hidden truths surfaced as the plot thickened and before too long I actually felt like I was in the room where each scene was unfolding. Each character, as you will discover, has a life journey riddled with unexpected twists and turns which all come together perfectly with the turning of each page.

Stella is a passionate woman with a big heart, known for her dedication, discipline and determination, all of which are clearly displayed on the pages of her book. I am humbled to find myself writing the foreword to this gripping novel, and I pray that God will continue to help you pen the gripping thoughts of your creative mind.

I honestly cannot wait to read the sequel.

~ Philip Donald Noel

PART
ONE

RUNAWAY

1

Today was her seventh birthday.

It had stopped raining, and the sun was shining nice and bright; she could see it through her curtains. She also caught a glimpse of the rainbow that hung beautifully in the sky.

It was meant to be a happy day. After all it was her birthday, but instead, all she wanted to do was hide; disappear under the duvet in her tiny little room.

Finally, she came out from beneath the sheets. Why did she feel so sore? Then, it all came rushing back to her, the picture of that brute and the weight of his body lying on top of hers.

It had been going on for some time, since the day she turned five, to be precise.

She had bottled it all up because he had threatened to kill her if she said a word to anyone, but apart from being scared she just wasn't sure if anyone would take her seriously. I mean, who would believe the words of a little girl with a vivid imagination?

Last night, however, was the last straw. She could keep quiet no more.

Finally, her mind made up; she decided to confront the situation the only way she knew how.

She managed to get to her feet, and gingerly walked down the staircase. With each step, she prayed that her path would not cross that brute unworthy to be called father.

In the kitchen, busy as usual, there she was; the woman she called mother.

Her mother looked unkempt, lonely and sad, and had recently taken to the bottle to drown her sorrows, to escape the reality of an unhappy marriage, but maybe that was just an excuse? Had this woman not noticed what was going on right under her nose?

She deliberately walked round and stood in front of her mother. For some silly reason she thought her mother would hug her, and lovingly ask, "What is the matter my darling daughter?" She thought her mother would finally notice that something was wrong. Instead, the woman frowned as she peered at her.

How dumb! Her young mind had expected too much. For a split second, she had forgotten that her mother was a cold hearted woman who lacked the ability to show affection of any kind, especially to her.

"Mother, please tell me, why is all this happening to me?"

"What is happening to you? What exactly is that supposed to mean? Go back to your room now." Her mother barked in her harsh voice.

Leah stood her ground and glared at her mother in open defiance.

"Leah, I said go to your room."

Leah could see the anger in her mother's eyes, but today she was not backing down.

"Mother, can you please tell me why this is happening? Why does father keep hurting me, and how come you never try to help?"

The woman squealed, her voice entirely devoid of compassion and love.

"Shut up and go back to your room right now. I do not want to hear another word from you."

Leah screamed back at her.

"I know you don't care, and I'm sure you don't even remember that today is my seventh birthday. All I want to know is why? Why does father keeping hurting me? Every night he does it, and you don't say anything."

Leah felt her mother's hard cold hand hit her full in the face. Shock combined with a rage she had never felt before swept through her. She turned, ran up the stairs, and locked herself in her room.

Leah sat on her bed and stared at the blank walls. She was in so much pain, but she couldn't cry.

No happy birthday, no hugs, no kisses, and definitely no 'I love you'. Somehow, all that was reserved for her older siblings. No one cared about her.

"What made her so different? What had she done wrong?" she asked herself.

Leah packed her drawing pad, her colouring pens and pencils, into her school bag, and waited until everywhere was quiet. Then she threw her coat over her pyjamas, quietly unlocked her door, and poked her head out.

The coast was clear.

Leah crept down the stairs and hurriedly walked through the front door. She did not look back. Leah just kept walking.

Leah was familiar with the route to the railway station because they had been there recently to see someone off. When she got there, she sat in the cold waiting room. She was starving, but there was nothing to eat, and even if there was, she had no money to buy anything.

With her head drooped, Leah began to cry. She cried and cried until her tears seemed to run dry. Then Leah felt something on her shoulder. With tired eyes, she slowly looked up and saw a lady, who wore the kindest smile Leah had ever seen, and a child standing beside her.

Much to Leah's surprise, the little girl looked very much like her; maybe a year or two older, but she could see the resemblance.

"Hello," Leah said, trying to use the hem of her pyjama top to dry her face.

"Hello to you too," the lady replied.

She sat down beside Leah, brought out a tissue, and used it to wipe the last of Leah's tears away.

"Now then, don't tell me that you're here all alone? Where are your parents? It is not safe for a child to be alone in a place like this. It can be very dangerous."

Leah looked at her through swollen eyes and a tear-stained face.

"Today is my seventh birthday, but no one cares. No one loves me. No one!"

The woman and the little girl wrapped their arms around her and hugged her for what seemed like forever.

Deep down inside Leah felt something pleasantly strange. For the first time in ages, she felt loved.

"Now, you cannot stay here on your own. I need to know who your parents are, and where you live so I can take you home," the lady said with a caring smile.

Leah could see the concern in her eyes, but there was no way she was going back to that house. The thought alone made her tremble.

"I do not have any parents," Leah whispered, looking away.

She knew the lady wouldn't believe her, but right now she would do or say anything to keep her from going back to that place of misery.

"Okay, you wait here with my daughter. I'll be back soon."

The lady opened the door and stepped out of the waiting room.

A few minutes later the door creaked open. It was the lady, but she was not alone. She had a policeman with her. Leah flashed an accusing glance at her. She should have known that this lady was too good to be true.

The lady walked over to Leah, crouched down, and took her hand. "This is Inspector Gerard."

Leah looked up at him but didn't say a word.

"Officer, I think this sweet little girl may have run away from home, and for some reason does not want to go back."

The Inspector sat down beside Leah, smiled and tried to hold her hand. Leah snatched her hand back as if she had been stung. Both the Inspector and the lady were taken aback by her reaction.

"So, do you live nearby? The Inspector asked.

Leah didn't say a word.

The Inspector continued.

"Who are your parents? Would you like me to call them so they can come by and take you home?"

2

There was no way Leah was going back to that house. The last people she wanted to see right now were her so-called parents.

Leah started bawling.

"Please don't cry," said the lady. "If you don't want to go home then you don't have to."

"Mummy, why can't she stay with us? We have more than enough room. She can even sleep in my room."

The little girl's face lit up. It was the first time she had said anything. She tugged at her mother's coat as if to emphasise her point then smiled at Leah.

"My name is Emily, by the way."

Leah gave her a shy wave as she wiped her tears away.

The situation seemed to be taking an awkward twist, and, following her daughter's suggestion, the lady wasn't exactly sure what to do.

A husky voice broke the uncomfortable silence. It was the Inspector's.

"Mrs Pearce, would you mind accompanying me to the station? I need to consult with my superior to confirm what action to take."

"No problem at all Inspector," she replied.

When they arrived at the police station, which was a five-minute walk away, the Inspector took a closer look at Leah. She seemed rather thin and frail as if she had been starved.

"Would you like something to eat?" You could see the pity in his eyes.

Leah nodded frantically.

Inspector Gerard invited Mrs Pearce and the two girls to sit down, then asked his secretary to order drinks and a bucket of Kentucky Fried Chicken.

Immediately Leah's eyes widened, and her mouth began to water.

Food at last!

While they sat down, Leah noticed some of the office staff whispering. It was obvious they were talking about her, but she couldn't care less. The only thing on her mind right now was food. She was starving.

She also caught Mrs Pearce staring at her. It was as if she had just realised that Leah was only wearing a nightie under her coat; a nightie which happened to be torn.

Embarrassed that she had been caught staring, Mrs Pearce, in a soft, kind voice, asked what Leah's name was.

"Annabel Leah. My name is Annabel Leah." Leah replied, deliberately leaving out her surname.

"What a lovely name. Do you have anything you can change into?"

Leah looked up at her and shook her head.

Leah's tummy was rumbling; the food still hadn't arrived. She was also beginning to feel sleepy.

"Keep your eyes open. Don't sleep. You cannot afford to sleep," Leah told herself.

An image of her being driven home flashed through her head. Immediately she opened her eyes wide.

Nobody was going to take her back to that house, and if she had to jump in front of a train to stop it from happening, then so be it.

Leah found herself thinking about her siblings.

Dora May was her eldest sister; they hardly spoke, but she was always there for her.

Her big brother Michael Jr, she called him Mike, always took her riding on his bike whenever he was around. He was the funny one. He always made her laugh.

Then there was Tricia. Both Trish, as she fondly called her, and Leah slept in the same room. That was until the day Leah turned five, and her father insisted that Trish should start sleeping in Dora May's room.

At the time Leah did not understand why. If only she had known.

The tears started welling up in her eyes again. She tried to brush them away with the back of her hand, but that didn't stop the flow. Even though Leah missed her siblings so much, there was no way she could let them know that she had run away from home.

Finally, the undeniable aroma of fried chicken filled the room.

For a moment Leah pushed all the misery to the back of her mind and tucked into the chicken with gusto.

She was faint with hunger and couldn't be bothered about what anyone thought of her bad table manners.

Then, out of nowhere, she heard the sound of voices singing. "Happy birthday to you, happy birthday to you, Happy birthday dear Annabel, Happy birthday to you!"

Leah couldn't hide her surprise; they were singing for her!

For the first time, Leah smiled.

Leah had eaten more than her fair share of the chicken, and now she felt nauseated.

She jumped up, ran to the washroom, bent over the sink and threw up.

After a few minutes, Leah lifted her head, cleaned up the best she could, and even though she still felt a bit sick, walked back to the reception.

Leah slumped into a chair.

Mrs Pearce, who had noticed that Leah was looking poorly, put her arm around her shoulders, smiled and asked if she was okay.

Leah looked at her dozily and nodded half-heartedly.

She has such kind eyes. They were a far cry from her mother's, Leah thought.

Then she saw Mrs Pearce's gaze shift downwards; her smile gradually replaced with a look of concern.

"What was the matter?" Leah wondered.

Then she looked. There was a wet blood stain between her legs.

Leah was shaken. The fear on her face was visible. Mrs Pearce cradled Leah in her arms; the tears rolled down her cheeks onto Leah's.

It was too much for little Leah; she couldn't hold it in any longer. It all came bursting out!

She told Mrs Pearce everything; how she had been abused since the age of five and had bottled everything up because she was afraid.

She told her about the man she called father; how he had been born into a very wealthy family; a family that happened to be part of an elite group that made taking care of their own their number one priority.

She told Mrs Pearce how he told her over and over again how no one would ever believe her if she blabbed; a lie that she had unfortunately believed.

Mrs Pearce listened to Leah's every word, and when the little girl was done she sighed.

She tenderly took Leah by the hand and led her to the washroom where she wiped the blood from between her legs, but did not go any further as she did not want to tamper with any evidence.

"Annabel, we are going to have to take you to the hospital. Are you sure you don't want to tell me who your parents are?"

Leah shook her head vehemently, and in a weak, shaky voice said, "I have no parents."

As they walked back from the washroom, Mrs Pearce whispered

in Leah's ear,

"You know I cannot keep you as my own as that will most likely get me into trouble with the authorities, but I am sure we can work something out."

Leah didn't exactly understand what she meant, but as long as she wasn't going home, she didn't care.

Emily smiled as Leah sat down.

There was just something about her smile that was so comforting; something about her smile that told Leah everything was going to be alright.

3

Inspector Gerard had been on the phone a while.

Leah held Mrs Pearce's hand and squeezed it tight. Her heart was pounding faster and faster. She could feel herself trembling all over. Her tummy started rumbling again, but this time around it wasn't hunger.

Thoughts raced through Leah's mind. Who was on the other end of the phone? Was he talking to her mum or her dad? Had the police finally found out who she was? Was she about to be taken back to that house of pain?

"I need you to come over as soon as possible."

Finally, Inspector Gerard hung up. He looked at Mrs Pearce and gave her the nod.

"You can take her home Mrs Pearce, and if possible could you please help change Leah into something a bit more presentable before we take her to the hospital?"

"Of course Inspector. Thank you so much."

Mrs Pearce was overjoyed.

As they left the station, Leah heaved a huge sigh of relief.

Mrs Pearce's house was in a nice, quiet neighbourhood.

The outside looked lovely, but inside was absolutely stunning!

Mrs Pearce asked for Leah's coat and hung it on the standing rack.

Then she took her upstairs to the bathroom, washed her face, her hands, her legs and her feet with a fresh flannel.

Leah wondered why she was going through so much hassle when a simple shower would have made things a lot easier; after all a nice, hot shower is what she really needed. It was later on, in the hospital, that it all made sense.

"Annabel, there is a dress that you can change into in there."

Mrs Pearce pointed to the adjoining room.

"I hope you like it."

She smiled and went downstairs.

Leah walked towards the room and peeped inside. There, on the bed, was a coral coloured dress. It was beautiful! She slipped into it and looked at herself in the mirror. Leah had gotten so used to wearing jeans and a tee shirt that she had all but forgotten how pretty she looked in a dress.

"You look amazing!"

Carried away by her new look, Leah had not seen Emily standing in the doorway.

"Oh, thank you Emily, and thank you so much for the dress."

Emily smiled. "I hope you like it?"

"I love it!" Leah exclaimed.

"Girls, it is time to go to the hospital. Are we ready?"

Emily ran excitedly down the stairs, but Leah wasn't too keen.

"Do I have to go to the hospital, Mrs Pearce?"

"Yes dear, we need to make sure that you are okay."

Mrs Pearce's reply was kind but firm, and Leah knew there was no wriggling out of this one.

Leah caught a whiff of that horrible odour.

"Why do all hospitals smell the same?" she wondered.

Mrs Pearce asked the girls to take a seat in the reception area while she spoke to a man wearing a white coat.

After a brief conversation, the man in white ushered Leah into a room.

Mrs Pearce noticed the bewildered look in her eyes.

"It is going to be alright Annabel."

She took Leah's hand and squeezed it reassuringly.

As they walked into the room, Mrs Pearce turned to her daughter.

"Sit tight darling, we will be back soon."

The doctor's examination was very uncomfortable, but Emily's mum never let go of her hand. As long as she was there, Leah felt safe.

When the doctor finished examining her, he looked at Mrs Pearce and nodded.

"I think I have everything I need."

Leah gently got up, adjusted her dress, and looked at Emily's mum.

"Can we go home now?"

"Yes, we can dear."

Emily had hardly opened the door to the house when the phone started ringing.

Mrs Pearce hurriedly picked it up and walked towards the kitchen.

"Hello."

Leah tried to listen to the conversation, but Mrs Pearce's voice was a faint whisper.

"Who could that be? "Why was she whispering?" "Did this have something to do with her?" The questions kept coming; the suspense was tearing her up inside.

After what seemed like an eternity, Mrs Pearce came out of the kitchen.

Leah could no longer control herself.

"Mrs Pearce, did that call have anything to do with me?"

"Annabel, I need you to sit down."

This was not looking good, Leah thought.

"That was Inspector Gerard. We need to go to the station."

Mrs Pearce paused.

"We need to find you somewhere to stay."

"Noooo!" Leah shook her head ferociously. "I want to stay here with you and Emily."

"I want you to stay with us, but it's not that straightforward Annabel. Child abduction is considered to be a severe crime."

"But... you didn't abduct me."

"I know my dear, but the law will not see it that way."

Leah threw herself on the ground and refused to get up.

Emily's mum pleaded with her to stand up and promised that no harm would come to her, but it was too late.

Leah felt betrayed. Had she made a mistake by choosing to trust this woman?

While Leah was still busy throwing a tantrum, Emily started crying.

"Mummy, why can't she stay with us? Why?"

"Not you too Emily. Please!" Her mum cautioned.

4

The shrill sound of the phone startled everyone into silence. Mrs Pearce hesitantly picked it up, looked at the girls as if to say, "No noise", and once again walked towards the kitchen.

Emily and Leah could hear her arguing about something not being proper, and how the whole situation was beginning to get out of hand.

Then the conversation ended, abruptly.

"That was Inspector Gerard. He would like to know what is holding us up."

The smile that so often lit up Mrs Pearce's face was gone, and the little hope Leah had faded away.

Leah knew Mrs Pearce cared for her, she never doubted it, but this situation was out of her hands.

It seemed only a matter of time before she would have to wave goodbye to Emily.

The thought made Leah's eyes swell up, but this time she just about managed to hold back the tears.

The entire reception area had changed. It looked nothing like the day before.

A television crew had set up their equipment, and someone who looked like a reporter was attaching a lapel mic to his jacket.

Both Emily and Leah clung tightly to Mrs Pearce as they waited for the Inspector.

Leah was so overwhelmed by everything going on around her that she didn't know when the tears started rolling down her cheeks.

Mrs Pearce crouched down, gently took Leah's wet face in her hands, and looked at her through tear-filled eyes.

"Annabel," she whispered softly, "I will not allow any harm to come to you. I will not let anyone take you home unless you wish to go. I just need you to trust me. Is that okay?"

Leah nodded, wrapped her arms around Mrs Pearce, and rested her wet cheeks on her shoulder.

At the same time, Leah felt a head rest on her back. It was Emily's!

Mixed emotions of guilt and love swept through Leah.

Before this morning Emily had her mum all to herself, but now she had to share her with a stranger, yet she wasn't jealous.

Each time Leah looked into Emily's lovely green eyes all she saw was love.

"Mrs Pearce, let me introduce you to Tim Brooks", said the Inspector. "He is a reporter with Channel 10."

A short, stumpy looking man wobbled over and shook Mrs Pearce's hand. The Inspector continued.

"The Department of Missing Persons and Channel 10 have a unique working relationship, and I believe they might be able to help us.

I would like Mr Brooks to ask Annabel a few questions, and also appeal to any family she might have out there to come over to the station. Is that okay with you?"

Mrs Pearce nodded, somewhat reluctantly.

It was obvious that she was not entirely comfortable with what was going on.

Inspector Gerard looked at Mr Brooks.

"Okay Tim, over to you."

Mr Brooks smiled as he sat across Mrs Pearce, Emily and Leah, and started the interview.

"So, which one of you is the runaway girl?"

There was an awkward silence. It was an attempt at humour, but it did not go down well.

Mr Brooks, blushing with embarrassment, tried to apologise, but it was too late.

Mrs Pearce gave the reporter a deep, stern look. Then, visibly shaking, voice raised, she gave the reporter a few choice words.

"What is going on over here?" the Inspector interjected.

"Well, I am sorry, but there is no way I am going to sit back and allow this man to make Annabel out to be some spoilt, attention-seeking child who has run away just to teach her parents a lesson. Who does he think he is?"

The Inspector was livid.

"Tim, I thought we discussed the sensitivity of this situation? Now, start the interview again, and please stick to the script. This child has been through enough as it is."

Inspector Gerard looked at Leah.

"Annabel, I am so sorry about what just happened, but don't worry, it will not happen again."

Mr Brooks' round face was still a flushed red as he attempted to restart the interview.

"Okay, let us wipe the slate clean and start again?"

"So Annabel, how old are you?"

"Seven."

"And, where do you live?"

Leah looked straight at Mr Brooks but didn't say a word.

"Do you know the names of your mum and dad?"

Still, Leah said nothing.

She could see that the reporter was getting frustrated, but there was no way she was going to answer that question.

"Okay Annabel, do you have any brothers, sisters, any relatives at all?"

"Yes, I do. I have an older brother and two older sisters. I also have grandparents, but they live far away."

Finally, a response. Mr Brooks could hardly contain his excitement.

"Good! Good! Could you tell me their names and where they live?"

"No."

"Annabel, please we need you to answer these questions. It's the only way we can help reunite you with your family; with your parents."

"I said I have no parents!" Leah shouted.

The office came to a standstill.

Mr Brooks stopped the interview.

"Cut. It looks like we are going to have to work with the little we have."

Leah was trembling all over. Mrs Pearce squeezed her hand and tried to calm her down.

She was the only one who knew what had happened; she was the only one who understood.

After the television crew had packed up, Mrs Pearce asked Inspector Gerard if she could have a word.

"Yes, of course."

They walked into his office, and he closed the door.

While Emily's mum and the Inspector were in the office, Leah saw a woman at the reception desk and heard her asking after Mr Gerard.

For some reason she reminded her of the Inspector; albeit a lot softer and more feminine, but also a bit older.

She took a seat opposite the girls and smiled.

Finally, the door to the Inspector's office opened.

Leah could tell by the look in his eyes that he now knew the whole story.

Inspector Gerard smiled at the lady who had walked in earlier.

"Ah, Hello Abigail."

"Mrs Pearce, please meet Mrs Abigail Tanner; the social worker

I spoke to you about. She has worked closely with the department for some time. Did I mention that she is my sister?"

That explained why they look alike; they were siblings! Leah smiled.

Mrs Tanner carried herself like an old-school matriarchal teaching hospital matron, but there was something about her; something that made you feel like she cared.

She just seemed kind and warm hearted.

It was too soon to jump to conclusions but in some way she was just like Mrs Pearce.

PART
TWO

JOSIE

It was six o'clock in the morning in Wellington, New Zealand. The sun was high, and the heat was building.

Sir Ian and his wife Lady Donna were watching the news in the comfort of their living room when a picture of a little girl appeared on the screen. It was their granddaughter.

The words that followed left them dumbstruck.

Donna turned to her husband, teary-eyed.

"Ian, what is going on? Have you spoken to Michael or Elsie lately? Did you know that little Leah had run away from home?"

"Calm down dear. Of course, I didn't know."

"Ian, what are we going to do?"

"Well, I guess we will have to call them and find out what happened. Hopefully, they will pick up the phone when we call."

There was a noise by the front door.

It was the paperboy posting the day's newspaper through the Doland letter hole.

Ian jumped to his feet and briskly walked to the door. He picked up the paper and hastily browsed through.

There, at the bottom right-hand side of the centre spread was little Leah's runaway story.

Compared to what they heard on TV, the story in the paper

was well detailed: when she ran away, who found her, the measures being taken to keep her safe. It was all there.

However, the part that disturbed Ian the most was that the authorities had taken Leah to the hospital because she had multiple bruises all over her body, and that there was also evidence she was malnourished.

Even though it was expressly stated that none of this had been disclosed by either the Police or Child Services, it did not offer Ian any comfort.

Ian had been ill for a while, and both Donna and he had decided that a change in habitat would do his health a lot of good. So, they relocated to New Zealand.

However, they both knew there was more to their move than Ian's health.

Seeing little Leah on the screen and reading about what had happened brought back memories.

"Is the past finally catching up with us?" Ian muttered to himself. "Michael has not changed his ways, Donna. Only God knows what he did to the poor child."

Donna sighed.

Ian always knew that Michael's mean streak would have consequences.

He remembered his son's escapades; how he often lied to draw attention away from himself, how he never hesitated to use his towering stature, and his reputation as a bully, to intimidate the other children.

Ian blamed himself.

He could have nipped it all in the bud at the time, but with his name and status at stake, he could not afford to have his son convicted of such trifle offences, which was how he viewed them at the time.

He remembered how he and Donna had decided that the best thing for the family was to send Michael away to a Catholic boarding school that was run by priests and reverend brothers.

Even there their son was a thorn in the flesh. He was rude to the teachers and treated his classmates as if they were his slaves.

"If he were not my only son I would have disowned him," Ian had told Donna on more than one occasion, but deep down inside he knew it wasn't that straightforward.

They hoped that one day Michael would change his ways, but it was hard to see how.

He had been suspended from school several times, and if not for the generous donations from the Doland Foundation, he would have been expelled.

After graduating at the age of twenty-two, Michael was offered a position at Doland & Associates, his father's law firm, which surprisingly he accepted.

At first, he seemed to enjoy it, then not too long after he decided that he wanted to get married and indulge in his passion for travelling and teaching classical medieval history and literature.

It was while he was teaching at St Magdalene's College that he met Josephine Kimberly.

6

Josephine Kimberly, fondly called Josie, was fifteen years old. She had long brown hair, blue eyes, a mildly freckled face and she almost always wore a smile.

Josie came from a good Christian home and was naturally friendly. She was a budding artist, and one of the top students in her class.

However, her greatest interest lay in classical literature, and she keenly looked forward to Michael's lectures.

Though Michael's reputation preceded him at St Magdalene's, Josie felt that he was misunderstood and that, even if he was sometimes ill-mannered, he should be given the benefit of the doubt.

To help in her own little way, she had encouraged Michael with short stories from the Bible in between lectures, and to the surprise of many, it seemed to work.

Michael began to smile more, and his behaviour towards his colleagues improved drastically.

Even his wife and children reaped the benefits as life at home became a lot more enjoyable.

However, that was all about to change.

It was Josie's sixteenth birthday, and she had gotten approval from the College authorities to have a small party on the last Saturday of the month.

She invited her classmates and asked Michael to come if he wasn't too busy.

Alcohol was not allowed, and drugs were a definite no go, and to ensure that they all obeyed the rules the girls would be supervised by the Matron, Mrs. Joanna Simpson, while the young men would be under the watchful eye of the Chaplain, Revd. Timothy Dean.

The party started at four on the dot. It was only going to last for three hours, so they had to make every second count. Revd. Tim kicked it off with a prayer:

"Dear Lord, I pray for these young ones and ask that You protect them. I also pray that You will expose every evil hidden in the hearts of those here today. Amen."

There was giggling and laughter, and the food went down a treat. Everything was just perfect until sometime after six.

"Josephine, come here. I want to dance with you," Michael bellowed.

Josie looked at him, a mixture of disgust and shock wrote on her face.

"What has come over you, Michael?"

He didn't bother answering. Instead, he grabbed Josie arm and pulled her to his chest.

"Michael stop it, you are hurting me," she cried.

Michael wasn't listening. He held her even tighter and then tried to kiss her.

She turned her face away, but Michael was determined to have his way.

Josie slapped him hard across the face.

Immediately his grip loosened. Josie freed herself from his grasp and ran out of the hall.

"Josie…, Josie…, where are you?" Josie didn't answer. She didn't have to.

The Matron could hear her sobbing. She followed the sound and found Josie crouched up in the corner of one of the classrooms.

Joanna sat down beside Josie and placed a comforting hand on her shoulder.

"I am so sorry about what happened. How are you feeling?"

"I'm...., I'm okay", Josie whispered. She flashed a half-hearted smile in an attempt to convince the Matron that she was alright, but Joanna could feel her shaking.

She offered to walk Josie to her room.

"Not to worry Miss, I'll be alright," said Josie.

"I know you will, but I'll walk with you anyway," Joanna insisted.

As they walked to Josie's room, Joanna told her that Michael had been escorted off the college premises by Revd Dean. They had also confirmed that Michael had managed to sneak two bottles of wine into the party which, though not acceptable, explained his tipsy behaviour.

"Here we are," said Joanna as they stood in front of the dormitory. Josie's room was on the ground floor; it was closest to the entrance.

"Are you sure you will be okay?"

Josie nodded. "Thank you, Miss."

Joanna smiled and waited until Josie locked the door behind her.

Josie knelt down by her bedside and pondered all that had happened. "Thank You Lord for giving me life, and for letting me see my sixteenth birthday," she prayed as a tear rolled down her cheek, "and please forgive me if I did anything wrong by having this party. All I wanted to do was have some fun with my friends."

Finally, she got up, had a shower, turned off her bedside lamp and crept under her duvet.

As Josie lay down, she felt a sense of relief as if something had been lifted off of her chest; before Josie knew it, she had drifted off.

It must have been around two o'clock in the early hours of the morning when a strange noise roused Josie from her sleep.

As she turned, she saw the silhouette of a man standing by the window.

Josie tried to scream, but a hard, rough hand quickly covered her mouth. He threw her duvet on the floor and pulled her out of bed, his hand still tightly clamped over her lips.

Josie kicked and struggled, tried everything she could to get loose, but he was too strong.

He opened the door and dragged her out.

She banged her feet on the floor hoping someone, anyone, would hear, but the carpet seemed to drown the sound. He pulled her through the front door to the nearby bushes. Was she dreaming?

Any hope of this being a dream quickly vanished when she heard his voice.

"No one slaps me and gets away with it."

Josie's eyes opened wide with horror. It was Michael! His breath reeked of alcohol.

She struggled with all her might, but it was in vain. She was no match for the power of this huge, intimidating figure.

Her strength gradually seeped away.

She tried to kick; she tried to fight, but now she could barely move her hands or feet. Too weak to struggle, Josie lay motionless.

Consumed by lust, Michael didn't notice Josie's limp body.

One hand still wrapped around her mouth, he tore her nightie, ripped off her underwear and raped her.

It had taken a while before he realised that she wasn't moving. Thinking she was dead, Michael panicked! He pulled up his pants, dragged her behind a nearby shed and ran.

It was Sunday morning, and everyone was getting ready to go to the chapel, but where was Josie?

She was usually the life and soul of Sunday mornings, but today she was nowhere to be found.

Lilly-Ann, Josie's roommate and best friend, had mistakenly fallen asleep in a friend's room the night before.

She had planned to sneak back in without waking Josie up, but as she approached the room, she knew something was wrong.

The door was slightly ajar, and the window was open. Josie's duvet was flung on the floor and her slippers miles apart. She was not in the bathroom, and her robe had not been touched.

Lilly-Ann ran to the Matron's office.

"Miss, Miss, I think something has happened to Josie."

After listening to Lilly-Ann's story, the Matron immediately gathered everyone together to search for Josie.

About thirty minutes had gone by when one of the college gardeners shouted, "Here, here, she's over here."

Josie lay lifeless in a bush beside a shed.

"Quick, call an ambulance."

The gardener picked her up and lay her down on the grass, while one of the pupils covered her with a blanket.

Revd Tim ran over, knelt down and checked Josie's pulse. It was weak, almost non-existent, but she was alive.

He held her hand and whispered, "Hold on Josie, don't give up."

It didn't look good, but as long as she was alive, there was hope.

The paramedics arrived in record time. "Her pulse is weak, and she has lost a lot of blood," one of them said.

They lifted her onto the stretcher and wheeled her into the ambulance.

Joanna held Josie's hand as the ambulance weaved through the traffic at top speed, sirens blaring.

She watched as the paramedics rushed Josie to the Accident & Emergency ward. If only she had stayed with her.

"Hello, Mrs Simpson." It was Josie's parents. Joanna had called them earlier and tried to break the bad news the best she could, then asked if they could meet her at the hospital.

Mrs Kimberly looked distraught; her eyes swollen, her face pale, while Mr Kimberly was trying to be strong for both of them, but he was obviously struggling.

"Hello, Mr and Mrs Kimberly…" She had hoped to give them the details of what had happened, at least the little she knew, but as Joanna looked at the couple, she had no words to say.

She hugged them both, and together they walked into the hospital's reception area, sat down and waited.

The police opened an investigation into the Josephine Kimberly rape case. They questioned almost everyone at the party and the name on everyone's lips was Michael Doland.

They hadn't brought Michael in for questioning as no one seemed to know his whereabouts.

Then there was also the small issue of him being Sir Ian Doland's son.

The Principal, Father Mike O'Brien, was having none of it.

"There will be no sacred cows," he insisted.

"But Sir, this is Sir Ian Doland's son we're talking about here," the investigating officer replied.

"You do know that he is one of the great pillars of this society, and personally the thought of Michael being involved in something like this is highly unlikely."

The Principal looked confused, and so did the accompanying constable.

"Officer, are you implying that a crime of this nature is the exclusive behaviour of someone from a less privileged background?"

The Principal was trying hard not to lose control.

"That is not what…" the officer tried to respond, but the Principal had heard enough.

"No one is above the law. Everyone at the party that evening must be questioned, and if that includes Sir Ian Doland's son, then so be it.

Also, from what I've been made to understand, and I'm sure you have heard it too, Michael Doland seems to be the prime suspect in this case. So, I would strongly advise that you do not let your personal feelings cloud your judgement."

The police officer bowed his head slightly, turned, and along with his constable, left the Principal's office.

Something strange had happened moments before the police officers left the Principal's office.

The constable had slipped a piece of paper into Father O'Brien's hand, while his senior officer was not looking.

As the officers closed the door behind them, Father O'Brien found himself hastily reading the words written on the crumpled piece of paper.

"Senior Officer Tony Pike is married to Sir Ian's cousin," it read.

"No wonder he wasn't keen on talking to the man," Father O'Brien muttered.

Right there and then, he picked up the phone and made a call.

There was a knock on the Principal's door.

"Come in."

Father O'Brien smiled as a tall, firmly built, white-haired middle-aged man stepped into his office.

"Gordon, thank you so much for coming. Please have a seat."

Mr Gordon Reece was a Police Chief Superintendent in a nearby county. He was also one of Father O'Brien's former parishioners.

Father O'Brien told Mr Reece about the situation he was facing.

"Yes, I read about it in the papers. Such a shame. How is the young girl doing?"

"Well, she is still in a coma and the doctor's haven't exactly given us anything to go on. All we know is that it is a touch and go situation."

"But how did Sir Ian's son get involved with this girl?"

Father O'Brien sighed.

"Well, he was on our support teaching programme. He taught here on a part-time basis. The boy seemed to be good with classical literature, and the students enjoyed his classes.

Josephine was one of his best students, and for one so young, she was one of the reasons why we kept him on.

Initially, we had drawn up plans to stop his classes because of his awkward, unfriendly nature, but Josie and a few other students had asked us to give the class, and Michael, another chance. Even some of the parents got involved in the petition. So, we did. After all, everyone deserves a second chance right?!

From the feedback it seemed like he was changing, becoming a better person, but as they say, 'a leopard can never change its spots'. If only I had listened to my gut instinct!

Gordon, for years I have done my best to make this school what it has become today, and just when I was thinking of retiring this goes and happens.

My God, where did I go wrong?"

Father O'Brien shook his head and looked heavenward.

"I understand how you feel Mike, but don't beat yourself up; this is not exactly your fault.

The young ones nowadays can be wild, and most times it has nothing to do with parental upbringing. From what I heard Sir Ian Doland is a decent, respectable gentleman. Unfortunately, his son isn't a chip off the old block.

You know, sometimes I envy you men of the cloth. Not having to deal with the heartache and pain that marriage and children can so often bring is a massive weight off your shoulders."

Gordon had a distant look in his eyes.

"Mike, you know this situation is outside my jurisdiction so I cannot make any promises, but I will see what I can do. I'll make a few calls and see what comes up."

"Thank you, Gordon. Just make sure you keep me posted. No pressure, but I am counting on you.

I haven't had a chance to have a proper conversation with Josie's parents yet, but when I do, I am sure they will want to know how an innocent birthday party turned into this nightmare."

"Not to worry Mike, as soon as I have something I will let you know."

8

It had been a month since Josie was rushed to St Margaret's Hospital, needing more than five pints of blood to keep her alive.

At one point the doctors thought they had lost her, but somehow she pulled through.

Even though she was still in a coma, it seemed the worst was over.

She was transferred to the Intensive Care Unit and monitored around the clock. As long as she was unconscious nothing could be taken for granted.

Josie's parents hardly left their daughter's bedside.

They kept vigil every night, taking turns to go home and look after the two little ones.

Their pastor had come over a few times to pray for Josie, and they had also asked friends and family to keep her in their prayers.

Though the Kimberlys were afraid of what might happen, they held on to their faith in God; hoping for a breakthrough, believing for a miracle.

Sitting there lost in thought, Angela was not aware of the nurse standing beside her.

"Sorry, I couldn't help but notice that you have been in that chair for quite a while. Would you like something to eat or drink?" the nurse asked.

"Oh, not to worry, I'm fine. Thank you so much… Nurse Heatherway," Angela replied tilting her head to look at the nurse's name badge.

"Mrs Kimberly…"

"Please, call me Angela."

Nurse Heatherway hesitated, then continued.

"Angela, you see if you don't eat you are going to end up falling ill, and then we are going to have another patient on the ward. It would also mean that you will no longer be able to look out for your daughter. Now, I'm sure we don't want that to happen do we?

Let's go to the canteen and grab something to drink. If Josie's situation changes, I'm sure a member of staff will let you know."

The tears were rolling down Angela's cheeks.

She wanted to believe that everything would be okay, but she was finding it hard to see the light at the end of the tunnel.

"Do you think she will come out of this coma? Will my Josie make it?"

Nurse Heatherway placed her hand on Angela's shoulder.

"I don't know, but your Josie is a tough girl. She has made it this far against all the odds, so don't give up just yet.

Why don't we grab that drink, and by the way you can call me Jessie."

Jessie handed Angela a mug of hot chocolate and sat beside her.

"Thank you, Jessie. I don't mean to be nosey, but how long have you worked here?"

"Well, this is my tenth year at St Margaret's. I trained here and continued working here afterwards. I can assure you that this hospital is one of the best in the country. Caring for patients is our number one priority.

Interestingly, we are also allowed to pray for patients and their families, with their permission of course." Jessie winked.

"Wow, that's great."

Angela hesitated for second.

"Do you mind if we prayed for my Josie?"

Right there in the cafe the two ladies held hands and asked God for a miracle; to wake Josie up and heal every part of her body.

There was a glow in Angela's eyes. Praying with her new found friend had given her a new lease of life. It had awakened her hope. Somehow she knew that God was going to heal her daughter.

Angela looked up and smiled at Jessie.

"Thank you so much."

9

Josie opened her eyes.

Holding her hand, head buried in the sheets, praying and crying at the same time, was her mum.

"Mum," Josie whispered.

Angela lifted her head, and her eyes met with a smile she hadn't seen in a long while.

"Josie!"

Angela leapt out of her bedside chair and screamed for joy, almost crushing her darling daughter in a loving hug.

Two nurses burst into the room.

When they heard Angela scream they had feared the worst, but to their amazement there was Josie awake, trying to sit up.

The nurses politely asked Angela to leave while they carried out a few basic checks on Josie.

Dr George Sirikipalan, a young man originally from Sri Lanka, walked into the room.

After spending a few minutes with Josie, he looked as surprised as the two nurses.

Josie had been in a coma for two months, and from what they could see, it was as if she was never unconscious.

Dr Sirikipalan smiled at Josie.

"Now this is a bit hard to comprehend. I guess I should have a word with your mum and dad."

"Maybe you should," Josie replied excitedly.

When the doctor opened the door, he saw Josie's parents pacing nervously up and down the corridor. He asked if he could have a word with them in one of the consulting rooms.

"Please take a seat Mr and Mrs Kimberly. Surprisingly, and I don't mean this in a bad way, Josie seems okay. Her vitals are normal; she's breathing perfectly well and so far we haven't noticed any memory lapses.

From my initial observation, it looks like she is in good shape which, considering everything she has been through is a miracle, but it is early days.

I am still waiting for a few more test results. Once we've got these, I will give you a more detailed assessment of Josie's health. Until then it would be better not to make any assumptions.

I'm sure you understand?"

"Yes, we do and thank you so much, doctor. By the way, any idea when the results will be ready?" Mr Kimberly asked.

"Hopefully that should be sometime tomorrow, but not to worry we will keep you informed," Dr Sirikipalan replied.

As the Kimberlys left the room, John turned to his wife. She had been unusually quiet.

"Are you alright honey?"

"I don't know John. I'm just a bit worried."

John gave his wife a long comforting hug.

"We are going to be okay." He whispered.

It was Monday morning, the day after Josie had come out of her coma, and Dr Sirikipalan was looking through Josie's results, which had just been handed to him.

He went through them, paused for a minute then went through them again. He looked puzzled.

"How did we miss this," he thought to himself.

Josie's parents had spent the night by their daughter's bedside.

John had woken up early and watched Angela as she slept. She looked exhausted; the sleepless nights had taken their toll.

Angela woke up and looked at her husband as if she had felt his eyes on her.

"John, hasn't the doctor called yet? They should know something by now."

Before John could say a word, Angela jumped up and walked out of the room. She stopped one of the nurses walking by and politely asked if there had been any update on Josie's test results.

"Mrs Kimberly, the doctor is looking through the results as we speak. I'm sure he will call you soon."

Angela felt that uneasy feeling again. Call it a mother's instinct, but somehow she knew that something wasn't right.

Different thoughts ran through her mind. She tried to ignore them, but they continually tormented her.

"Lord, please help my daughter," she prayed under her breath.

Finally, Dr Sirikipalan accompanied by nurse Heatherway came into Josie's room.

"Mr and Mrs Kimberly, if you don't mind could you please follow me."

A few minutes later the couple found themselves sitting in the same seats they sat in the day before.

With nurse Heatherway standing behind them, the Kimberlys listened intently to what the doctor had to say.

"Mr and Mrs Kimberly, we have examined Josie thoroughly, and all I can say is that her recovery is nothing short of miraculous. Her organs are functioning normally, her bruises have healed well.

There doesn't seem to be any significant brain damage or memory loss.

At the moment she doesn't remember what happened that night, but this is not unusual after such a traumatic event. That memory will most likely return with time.

Personally, the longer she remained unconscious, the more I feared the worst, but witnessing incredible feats like this reminds we medics that there is a higher power out there who can do things that we deem impossible."

Dr Sirikipalan changed his sitting position, cleared his throat and looked directly at the couple.

"There is, however, one thing. You are both aware of what happened to your daughter that night."

He paused.

"Well, after running the tests again I can confirm that your daughter is pregnant."

"Noooo!" John slammed his fist on the doctor's table, anger written all over his face. He had become an entirely different person, and it was painful to watch.

"How come you just found out about this?" he shouted, "We have to abort the baby; there are no two ways about it."

Until now all Angela had done was listen to what the doctor had to say. She had tried to hold back and not say anything, but her husband's words had pushed her over the edge.

She looked at him like he had gone crazy. She shook her head in dismay and disbelief.

"John, stop it!" she screamed.

All of a sudden John looked like a wild animal that had been forcibly tamed. He lowered his head, embarrassed and ashamed.

Still looking at her husband, Angela spoke in a quiet voice.

"I knew something wasn't right; I felt it yesterday when Josie woke up. It's hard to explain, but somehow I know this is not a coincidence. We need to respect Josie's wishes.

If she decides to keep the baby, I will stand by her and love the little one as if it were my own. After all, none of this is the child's fault."

The fight had left John, and the tears were flowing freely from his eyes.

"I don't know what came over me. What was I thinking? I am so sorry. Please forgive me."

Angela held John's hand and looked at him through teary eyes.

"It's okay John, you did nothing wrong. You only did what any caring father would have done."

"If it's alright, could I please be excused? I would like to see my daughter."

Angela got up and walked out of the room.

John turned to Dr Sirikipalan and apologised for the way he had behaved.

"I understand Mr Kimberly. News like this can be very distressing. I would, however, suggest that we try and focus on Josie from now on."

John nodded in agreement.

"Does Josie know about the baby yet?"

"Not yet. I thought I should tell you first, being her parents. She is going to need your full support."

John sighed.

"How long do you think it will be before she can be discharged?"

"Well, maybe tomorrow, but it will depend mostly on how she takes the news about the baby."

"Thank you, doctor. Angela and I are truly indebted to you, and the St Margaret's staff, for the care and attention given to our daughter. We will never forget it."

"You're welcome, Mr Kimberly. I'm just glad that we were able to help in some way."

Nurse Heatherway was still in Josie's room when Angela walked in.

"Hello, Jessie."

"Hello, Angela."

"Where is Josie?"

"She's taking a shower at the moment."

"I guess you know about the baby?"

"Yes, I do. I'm so sorry.

"It's alright," Angela sighed. "I'm just worried about my little girl. I don't know how she's going to take this. What do you think?

"Well, it's hard to say really. I know that Josie is a fighter, but she's still only sixteen years old. All you can do is let go and let God.

"I guess you're right Jessie."

Angela looked resigned. How she wished she could do something to ease her daughter's pain.

"Anyway, I have decided to take time off work so I can look after Josie once she is discharged. We will just have to take it one step at a time."

"If it's alright with you, could I come by from time to time to help out?"

"I would appreciate that. I get the feeling I am going to need all the help I can get."

Angela slumped into the chair beside Josie's bed.

"You know, I keep asking myself, "Where did we go wrong?"

John and I have always wanted the best for Josie. It's one of the reasons why we sent her to St Magdalene's College, one of the best Christian schools around, in the first place, but see where that got us."

Jessie knelt down beside her and placed her arm around Angela's shoulders.

"There is evil everywhere under the sun. The heart of man is deceitful and desperately wicked, but I know that the person who did this to your daughter will not escape God's judgement."

10

Father O'Brien was pacing up and down his office when the phone rang. It was Gordon.

"Hello Gordon, any news on Michael Doland?"

"Not yet Mike. My source told me that his wife claims not to have seen him since the day before the attack, and when we called Sir Ian he said he hasn't spoken to his son in ages. But not to worry Mike, we will find the Doland boy, and if he is guilty, justice will prevail."

"I was thinking of calling Sir Ian myself. He and his wife have got to know something."

"I don't think that's a good idea. We need to be patient. Michael can't hide forever. He's going to slip up soon, and when he does, we are going to be there to catch him."

Father O'Brien's sighed.

"Okay Gordon, I'll leave it with you."

Gordon was about to drop the phone when he remembered something.

"By the way, how is the young girl doing?"

"Well, I was told that she is out of the coma and could be discharged soon, which is fantastic news. However, I got the feeling that wasn't the whole story."

"My friend, I know you're a man of the cloth, but the hospital staff are not obliged to tell you everything. There is still something such as patient confidentiality you know."

"Yeah, I know. I just wish I could do something to help."

"You just keep praying Mike. Keep praying."

"Okay Gordon, I'll keep praying."

While Dr Sirikipalan was advising the Kimberlys on their daughter's aftercare, there was a knock on the door. It was nurse Heatherway.

"Josie is awake."

As they walked to Josie's room, the doctor turned to the Kimberlys.

"Please let me do the talking."

John and Angela nodded in agreement.

"Hello, Josie. How are you feeling?"

"I'm fine doctor, but I feel a bit nauseated, and my legs seem to cramp every now and then. Is that normal?"

Dr Sirikipalan knew that the time had come to break the news to Josie.

"Josie, we have carried out some tests, and I am glad to say that there is nothing to worry about."

Josie wasn't convinced. She knew there was something he wasn't telling her.

"But?" she asked, looking straight into his eyes.

The doctor cleared his throat.

"Even though you have no major injuries you…"

"What is it, doctor? Am I infected with something? What is it? Just tell me."

Angela tried to calm her daughter down.

"Darling…"

"Mum, what isn't the doctor telling me?"

She held her daughter's hands.

"Darling, just relax and listen to what the doctor has to say."

Dr Sirikipalan continued.

"Josie, you are pregnant!"

"That's impossible!" Josie screamed.

She looked at her parents waiting for them to tell her that it was a mistake, but the tears in their eyes said it all.

"But, how? How?" she cried, looking at her mum.

Angela held her daughter tight to her bosom and tried to console her.

It was all in vain.

Josie wanted to run away and hide. She wanted the earth to open and swallow her up. The more the reality dawned on her the harder she wept.

Then Josie jerked free of her mother's embrace and sat up.

She sat there motionless staring into space through tear-filled eyes.

John and Angela looked at Dr Sirikipalan hoping he could offer an explanation for what was happening, but he said nothing.

Finally, a bemused John could take it no longer.

"Doctor, what is happening to my daughter?"

"I'm not sure, but she might be remembering something."

The doctor was right.

As the tears rolled down Josie's cheeks, she remembered everything. Michael trying to kiss her,… her slapping him,… talking to the Matron,… the intruder in her room,… trying to scream,… being dragged into the bushes,… her nightie being ripped off,… being too exhausted to move,… the stench of alcohol on his breath as he pinned her down, and… She remembered everything!

"Michael!" she whispered under her breath. "It was Michael!"

There was perfect silence; you could hear a pin drop.

The police, who had been called in to take a statement from Josie, had just left.

Josie sat on the bed looking endlessly at the sheets, holding her head in her hands. Her dad had looked a bit reluctant; almost as if he didn't want her to give her statement.

Her mum, on the other hand, had encouraged her to tell the police everything, saying that it would help get it off her chest.

In hindsight maybe she should have waited a little because now she was finding it hard to get it out of her head.

She replayed the scene over and over and over again.

"Why me?"

After a while, Josie lifted her head and looked at everyone in the room.

"Thank you, doctor, for all that you and the staff have done for me. I really do appreciate it."

She turned to her parents.

"Mum, dad, I don't know what to do right now, but I will pray and ask God for His will and hope that I have the strength to do what He says."

They were all amazed at her composure and comportment, but Angela was not at ease with this sudden, dramatic change.

A few minutes ago she was confused and broken; now she was like a pillar of strength with an amazing will. Angela wasn't buying it.

John took his daughter's hand.

"Sweetheart, whatever you decide to do we will stand by you, but make sure you don't rush into anything."

"Thanks, dad. I know I can always count on you and mum."

Angela pushed her daughter's wheelchair towards the hospital entrance, giving Josie a chance to say her goodbyes to the staff and well-wishers. Seeing Josie smile after all she had been through was inspiring, and it was no surprise that some of the hospital staff got rather emotional.

As they approached the door, Josie thought about what her new life would be like. Would she ever be able to live a normal life again?

When John saw them exit the hospital he jumped out of the car, opened the door and helped his daughter into the backseat.

"I can walk dad!" she said.

"I know you can; that's why I'm only holding your hand and not carrying you."

They all burst into laughter. The tone was set for the journey home.

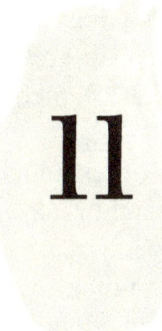

11

The Kimberlys arrived to find that some of the church members had organised a surprise reception to welcome Josie home.

Even though Josie was grateful, she had no intentions of being the focus of anyone's pity.

Rather than sit down and listen to depressing words, Josie lit up the place with her lovely smile. She served the tea and coffee, gave out the cakes and scones, and refused to discuss what happened to her with anyone.

After everyone had gone Josie helped tidy up the cups and saucers and was almost about to start washing them when her mum insisted that she sit down, and get some rest.

Josie went upstairs and stood in front of the door to her room.

The last time she stepped in here she was a happy fifteen-year-old, without a care in the world.

All that had changed.

Finally, she turned the knob and opened the door. It looked exactly the same.

Josie sighed, knelt down by her bedside and cried.

She felt so tired. The burden was just so heavy, and she couldn't see how anyone could help her carry it.

Josie knew her mum and dad would do the best they could, but no one could wipe away the pain and shame.

Amidst the tears, she asked for God's help and drifted off to sleep.

While she slept, Josie had a dream.

She saw the heavens open up and the angels descending and ascending, each carrying what seemed like a bouquet of flowers which they left by her side.

Then she noticed some other angels singing songs of praise while she cheered and clapped her hands. She felt lost in the warm embracing arms of her heavenly Father.

She heard a soft, tender voice say to her, "My dear child, I love you. This unfortunate incident will not thwart my purpose for your life. Trust Me and I will guide you in all your decisions. I promise that I will never leave you nor forsake you. The child you are carrying is appointed to great things but be careful to whom you entrust her."

Josie woke up.

She was no longer tired, nor did she feel sick.

She got up, washed her face, changed and went downstairs.

John saw her coming down the stairs and asked how she felt.

"I feel refreshed actually. I also had the most beautiful dream."

Josie paused for a few seconds.

"Dad, I want to tell you and mum that I will be keeping the child."

John couldn't believe his ears.

"Josie, have you thought about school, your career, your future? You need to think this through before you make a decision my dear."

"John!"

Angela seemed to appear from nowhere.

"This is her decision, and like you said, we will stand by her."

John looked away as he tried to hide his anger.

Josie did not want her parents to get into an argument over her; that was never the plan.

"Dad, remember granddad left me a tidy sum without stipulating my age of inheritance? Well, I was thinking of using part of this for my home studies, and also to pay for a nanny to help out with the baby. Is that okay?"

"Josie, this has nothing to do with the money. I just don't think you're thinking straight at the moment."

"Dad, I know you don't agree, but I believe that this is what I am supposed to do, and there is no way I can do it without your support."

Angela could see that this conversation was not going to end well.

"Josie, give your dad and I some time to think about this. I'm sure we can work something out."

Slowly, Josie turned and went up to her room.

John and Angela spoke at length about Josie's intentions.

He wasn't convinced that his daughter had thought it through. Left to him she didn't understand the implications, and how this one decision could affect her entire future.

Angela agreed with her husband, but what would happen to the baby?

"So, since you don't want Josie to keep the baby, I guess you want her to have an abortion?"

The question caught John off guard; he hadn't thought of it that way.

"Darling, I am not excited about our daughter having this baby either, but if we persuade her to have an abortion, I don't think she will ever forgive us.

Apart from that, we haven't even stopped to ask where God is in all this."

The more she spoke, the more John could see sense in what she was saying, and even though he hated to admit it, she was right.

"John, instead of us trying to think this through maybe we need to stand together in prayer and ask for the Father's will to be done."

Angela could feel the pain he was going through; she could

see the hurt in his eyes, but she knew that he knew that they were going to have to trust God in this situation.

The silence in John's study was tangible; you could almost touch it.

John stared out of the window, into the distance pondering the words his wife had spoken.

"Angela, you're right. We need to pray."

Mr and Mrs Kimberly went down on their knees, held hands and together they prayed for God to take control, and have His way.

When they eventually stood up, they had heard no specific word from God, but they both knew that somehow God was going to turn things around for good.

Still in her room, Josie thought about her siblings; her little sisters, Lois and Daphne who always looked up to her, and her big brother Bruce who always looked out for her.

Being raped, now pregnant and soon to be a teenage mother, it felt like she had let them all down.

How she wished her parents had talked her out of having that blasted party.

Unfortunately, there was no turning back the hand of time.

All Josie could do was hold on to what God had told her in the dream.

There was a knock on Josie's door.

It was her parents.

That dreaded moment had finally arrived.

John cleared his throat.

"My dear Josie, I'm sorry about earlier on. I was so caught up in what I thought was the right thing to do that I forgot about what you must be going through.

Anyway, your mum and I have given it some thought, and we will stand by whatever you choose to do."

Josie jumped up and hugged her dad, drying her teary eyes on his shirt.

"Thank you, dad. I love you so much!"

Then remembering that her mum was also inside the room, she looked up at her and smiled.

"I love you too mum."

Angela smiled and wrapped her arms around them both.

"I know you do."

As John and Angela were about to leave their daughter's room, she said in little more than a whisper.

"There's one last thing I wanted to ask for."

Both her parents were afraid to look back. What could it be this time?

"What's that Josie?" Angela asked.

"Do you mind not telling Bruce, Lois and Daphne about the baby just yet; I would like to do that myself when the time is right."

PART
THREE

MEMORY LANE

12

"Would you like me to bring your coffee upstairs or are you coming down?" Donna asked.

Ian was quiet.

As he looked at his wife memories of how she had spoilt Michael rotten rushed through his mind. What made it worse was that she seemed to be in complete denial.

For some reason, she believed there was no way her dear son could be responsible for the terrible things he was always being accused of.

Finally, Ian asked Donna to sit down, ushering her to the chair beside his.

"I have been thinking about Michael a lot lately."

Donna was about to say something, but Ian held his hand up.

"Please, just hear me out. It's about time we confronted this issue once and for all. We never denied Michael anything. He was a pampered child, and you my dear had a lot to do with that."

"Well, there you go. It's all my fault as usual, but don't forget that Michael is our only son. He was bullied in school too, remember? So, why should he be the scapegoat, blamed for the failings and weaknesses of the others?"

The look in Ian's eyes spoke volumes.

"Just listen to yourself! Whether we like it or not we must accept some responsibility for the way the boy has turned out.

Personally, I have concluded that we made a terrible mistake which has now come back to haunt us."

There was a brief silence.

"So, you believe that Michael would abuse his own child? Well, I refuse to believe that."

"There you go again, Donna. Why do you think the little girl told the police that she has no parents? Do you actually believe that those bruises on her body appeared by magic?

There we were thinking that marriage, and having children would change him. We were wrong!

And by the way, I'm not just blaming you. All I am saying is that we need to admit that when it comes to Michael we failed.

We should have been stricter with him; we should never have turned a blind eye.

I think we need to go back to England."

Donna was taken aback.

"Why? What do you plan to accomplish by returning to England? I prefer it here, and you know the weather over there will not do your health any good."

"Donna, we need to stop thinking about ourselves for once. There is a little child over there who needs us. Do you not think it is about time we tried to put things right?"

Donna took a long hard look at her husband, got up, and walked angrily out of the room.

Ian remembered that mild winter afternoon when Chief Superintendent Gordon Reece came to see him at his English country home.

Gordon Reece had contacted Ian asking if it was possible to meet with him.

Sensing the urgency in the policeman's voice, Ian had invited him over.

"Please come in," said the butler. "Sir Ian is expecting you."

"Thank you."

Gordon followed the butler down the corridor to a room which looked like a study.

"Good afternoon Sir Ian."

"My dear chap, you sounded rather disturbed over the phone. What is this matter of great urgency?"

"Well Sir, I was wondering if you had heard about the incident that occurred at St Magdalene's College.

A young girl was attacked on the College grounds, and the suspect is still at large."

"And, if I might ask, what does this have to do with me?" Sir Ian looked bemused.

"We have it on good authority that your son Michael was involved. Unfortunately, his whereabouts since the day of the attack is unknown."

Just before Sir Ian could respond there was a knock on the door. It was Lady Donna.

"This is Chief Superintendent Gordon Reece my dear. My wife, Donna."

"It is a pleasure to meet you, ma'am."

Lady Donna smiled and bowed her head slightly.

"He is here about Michael. It seems our son may have had something to do with an ugly incident at St Magdalene's."

Lady Donna did not hesitate in her response.

"Chief Superintendent, Michael is a married man with children, children he loves dearly. I can assure you that my son would never be involved in a crime of such nature."

"Lady Donna, Michael has been identified as the prime suspect by the victim. Unfortunately, we have been unable to question him as no one seems to know his whereabouts.

All I am saying is if he is innocent it would be advisable for him to speak to the police so he can clear his name."

"I know exactly what you are saying officer, and all I'm saying is you are wasting time looking in the wrong place.

My son is a gentleman, and like I said, he would never be involved in a crime of this nature."

Lady Donna's statement had an air of finality about it.

Mr Reece knew when he was no longer welcome.

"Well, I guess I will be on my way then. Thank you for your hospitality."

Sir Ian escorted Chief Superintendent Reece to the door.

"I understand, you have a job to do. I will be sure to let you know if I see or hear from Michael, and please forgive my wife for being a bit offhand with you. I am sure you know a thing or two about the mother-son bond."

"Oh, I understand Sir Ian."

Both men laughed.

When Ian opened the door to his study, he found Donna pacing up and down, still fuming at the intrusion.

"How dare he come into our house and accuse my son of such a crime."

"I don't remember hearing him accuse Michael of anything. He was only doing his job. If Michael is a suspect, then he needs to make himself available for questioning. That is the right thing to do."

"I will not allow anyone spoil my son's reputation. What will people think if a rumour like this was to spread?"

"Why do you care so much about what other people think? Michael is my son too, but if he had anything to do with this brutal attack on that young girl, then he will have to suffer the consequences. It is a serious offence which should not be condoned by anyone."

Donna gave her husband a stern look and stormed out of the study.

The Butler picked up the ringing phone.

"A phone call for you, my Lady."

"Hello, who is this?"

"It's me, mum."

Donna's voice suddenly turned to a faint whisper.

"Where are you, Michael? The police have been here looking for you. I heard they went to your house and Elsie told them she had not seen you since the day of the attack. She even said she was considering reporting you as missing. What have you done?"

"Mum, I did nothing. It was consensual. The girl was coming on to me like crazy. It was her idea for us to make out in the nearby shed. I'm telling the truth mum; I did nothing wrong."

"The Police reported that the girl was only sixteen years old. Michael, you know that having sex with a minor is a crime. What were you thinking son?"

"I will go to the police and tell them my side of the story."

"You will do no such thing! Have you considered the impact this will have on Elsie and the children, not to talk about our family and circle of friends?

Come to the house as soon as you can. We need to talk this over with our solicitor, do you hear me?"

"Yes, mother. I will see you tomorrow at around four o'clock. What is father saying about all this?"

"Leave your father to me; I will handle him. You need to worry about your wife and kids."

Ian opened the door to his study just in time to catch Donna replacing the receiver. He knew from the guilty look on her face that she had spoken to Michael.

"That was the prodigal wasn't it?"

"Yes, it was Michael."

"Did he confess?"

"To what exactly? You have judged our son already without even hearing his side of the story. What kind of father does that?"

"My dear, you need to get your head out of the clouds? Deep down inside you know what Michael is capable of, so why do you keep closing your heart to the truth?

Let me tell you now; I will not play a part in any conspiracy to shield him. If he is guilty, then he will face the consequences.

Have you even given any thought to the young girl whose life will never be the same again?"

Ian turned and walked into the garden. It was the only place where he seemed to find peace nowadays.

He couldn't help but wonder how much his wife had changed over the years. She seemed nothing like the lovely, caring woman he had married years ago or had she always been like this, and he was the one too busy to notice?

Ian had showered Donna with love and indulged her every whim, but he had failed to see that their status in society made her feel she was better than everyone else.

Ian was reluctant to admit it, but the truth was his wife had become a horrible snob, and unfortunately it was partly his fault.

But, what could he have done? As a young qualified lawyer working in his father's chambers, he was only carrying on the family tradition; every first-born male in the family was required to be a lawyer.

Some of his forebears had been prominent lawyers; some the best judges in the land, while others had taken their seat in the House of Parliament. Whatever the case, they were the movers and shakers of society.

At the age of sixty-two, it felt as if he was carrying the burden of the whole world on his shoulders.

Even though he still had so much to give, Ian was about to retire because he realised that the workload he had carried for years, mainly to please his now deceased father, had taken its toll on his health.

As the Chief Judge in charge of the Family Division of the Courts of Justice, retirement should have been the last thing on his mind, but he soon realised that if he wanted to stay alive, he would have to step down. The demand was just too much.

He also believed that the new laws regarding family issues were in direct contrast to both his Protestant and Catholic upbringing, an issue he had recently discussed with his parish priest, the Right Reverend Ted O'Connor.

13

The butler walked into the garden.

"Father O'Connor is in the living room, Sir."

What a coincidence, he thought. Or was it?

"Father O'Connor, to what do I owe this pleasure?"

"Ian, can we talk somewhere private?"

"Yes, of course."

Ian led Father O'Connor into the garden. This wasn't a social visit.

"How can I be of service Father?"

"Well, I had a phone call from Father Mike O'Brien, the Principal of St Magdalene's College. I believe you know him?"

"Yes, I know Father Mike. What did he say, and why are you telling me this?"

"Ian, I have always considered you to be a friend. I still remember the day you decided to go to Cambridge to study Law, and I picked Exeter to study Theology and Philosophy purely out of curiosity.

I never really thought I would end up being a priest, not to talk of being your parish priest. It all seems like a coincidence, but our Lord works in mysterious ways.

Anyway, Father Mike told me that your son attacked a young girl at St Magdalene's about two months ago.

Apparently, she woke up from her coma, and confirmed that Michael was her attacker. I was shocked when Father Mike told me.

We both know about Michael's wild streak and how it can occasionally get out of hand, but this!

Even Michael would not go this far. Have you heard from him lately?"

"Father O'Connor, if you are asking if I have heard from Michael, then the answer is 'no'. However, I think he may have spoken to his mother earlier on today."

"Ian, you know that if Michael is found guilty, the integrity of the Doland name will come crashing down like a pack of cards?"

"Well, I guess we will have to cross that bridge when we get there. As much as I abhor what that poor girl has suffered, I think we owe it to Michael to at least hear his side of the story, do we not?"

"True. Anyway, I just came to tell you what I heard."

"Thank you very much, Father. I appreciate your concern."

As Ian walked back to the garden, it dawned on him that Father Ted had not asked after his wife; he had not even indicated any intention of speaking to her about what he heard.

He knew only too well that most of the parishioners in their local church felt that his wife was a big snob who only hobnobbed with the rich and mighty.

Unfortunately, it was true. Donna no longer cared about those who lacked status and riches, but in hindsight, maybe it was not all her fault.

Donna was an only child, and her parents indulged her generously; she was one of the debutantes of her set.

They had met at a garden party at a mutual family friend's house.

Ian had been amused at her antics, looking at him from under her brows while at the same time flirting with other young men at the party.

He felt challenged by her impulsive behaviour and decided to rise to the occasion by asking her to dance with him.

Ian was surprised to find out later that she had already made enquiries about who he was, who his parents were and what he did for a living.

Usually, that would have set the alarm bells ringing, but he let it go and decided to play along.

She introduced herself as Donna King, a History student at Bristol University who, at the time, was engaged in cataloguing artefacts at the Victoria and Albert Museum.

Donna took him over to meet her parents.

Her mum seemed like a simple, quiet lady. She was stunningly beautiful, but for some reason, she looked out of place. Even though she was decked out in the most exquisite of gowns and expensive jewellery, she somehow did not fit in. She looked like she would have been happier in an arts or cookery class.

Donna's father, on the other hand, was a loud, boisterous character who liked making his presence felt. From what Ian could see, Donna had inherited her father's personality, but her beauty came from her mother.

They walked back to their seats and were soon engaged in conversation, which was mostly one sided as Ian let Donna do most of the talking.

As the party progressed, Ian noticed that Donna's mother, Mrs Tessa King, was sitting all alone with a faraway look in her eyes. He went over to talk to her, and as they spoke, he developed an affinity for her.

Surprisingly, Ian found himself imagining what she would be like as his mother-in-law.

14

Ian and Donna had a whirlwind courtship, and even as Ian thought about it, he still wasn't sure who proposed or swept the other off their feet.

Soon marriage was knocking on the door.

He remembered how Donna had tried to boss him around from the day they tied the knot, but he was not having any of it.

When the twins, Jennifer and Winifred, who they fondly called Winnie, were born Ian realised that Donna was not the domesticated, caring mother he had hoped she would be.

She tended to lash out at the girls at the slightest irritation, often reminding them of how their birth had messed up her figure.

If not for the caring nanny who most of the time kept the twins out of their mother's way, the girls may not have grown up to be the beautiful, well-mannered ladies they were today.

At the time, Ian was an upcoming lawyer who, though working in his father's city chambers also took on personal jobs from the government.

He found himself having to work away from home during the week because they lived in the village of Abbot Langley, and it was not practical to commute to work every day. He did, however, try his best to spend every weekend with the family.

Finally, when he could afford it, Ian bought a decent family house in London. The main reason why he had chosen the location was so that Donna would not miss out on the life she was used to.

When they relocated, Donna threw herself into morning coffees, afternoon teas and night parties with her group of friends.

They all dressed alike and acted as if they could not live without each other.

Unfortunately, they all had a nasty habit of talking behind each other's back.

One night, about five years after moving to London, Ian noticed that Donna was unusually quiet.

After much persuasion, she finally told him that she was pregnant.

Abortion was not an option as she saw herself as a good Roman Catholic girl. So, as the days went by she made everyone in the house miserable with her bickering and haughty manner, taking out most of her frustration on her daughters.

The only time she seemed happy was when she was gossiping on the phone with her so-called friends.

As the due date drew near, she moved to her parent's country estate. She did not really like it there, but as long as she was pampered, she did not mind. On that estate, Donna was treated like a queen!

Ian remembered the night he received a call from Donna's parents telling him that his presence was needed at the hospital.

He jumped up, washed his face, dressed up and drove like a mad man. He reached the hospital, which was not exactly a stone throw away, in record time, and rushed to the reception to ask about his wife.

While he was talking to the nurse on duty, he saw his mother in law sitting in a corner having a cup of tea.

"Oh Ian, that was fast!"

She seemed surprised to see him.

"Anyway, thank God you're here. After dinner your wife started complaining of cramps, then she started screaming and trashing the house. So her father decided to call an ambulance."

"Has the doctor seen her yet?"

"Yes, he has. Oh look, there he is."

Ian turned to see the doctor and Mr King walking towards them.

"Doctor, this is my son in law, Ian Doland," she said.

"How are you, Sir?"

The doctor shook Ian's hand.

"I'm alright," Ian stuttered. "How is my wife? Is she okay? Can I see her?"

"We gave her some medication to calm her down, but she's fine. You can go in and see her if you like."

Ian entered the room.

As she saw him, she started wailing, blaming him for the condition she found herself in. In an attempt to comfort her he found himself almost being strangled.

Ian tried to take her hands off his neck, and finally, after a bit of a struggle, he managed to break free of his wife's firm grip.

He held her hands, took a few seconds to get his breath back then looked into her eyes.

"Donna, you are going to be fine."

His words seemed to have the desired soothing effect.

Donna immediately calmed down and like a spoilt child said, "I never, ever want to get pregnant again."

"That's okay by me," Ian whispered.

He held her in his arms until she finally fell asleep. He kissed her on the forehead and quietly left the room.

That night Ian decided to sleep in the hospital, while Donna's parents returned home.

Ian sat up, rubbed his eyes and wondered what he was doing in the hospital waiting room. He had not realised how tired he was.

Anyway, it did not take long for him to remember why he was here.

He jumped up and ran to his wife's room.

It was empty!

As he came out, he saw a nurse talking to the doctor he met the night before.

They both smiled when they saw him.

"Congratulations Mr Doland, you are the father of a bouncing baby boy," the doctor said. "Nurse, please take Mr Doland to the labour room."

Ian could not hide his disappointment as he spoke to the doctor.

"Why didn't someone wake me up when my wife went into labour? That was the reason why I spent the night here in the first place."

"You looked pretty exhausted, so I told them not to wake you up. I apologise for that."

When Ian walked into the labour room, Donna was being cleaned up, while the baby was in the arms of the midwife.

He rushed to his wife's side and cuddled her.

"Oh Ian, it's a boy. I have always wanted a boy. Look at him, isn't he handsome. He looks just like my father."

Ian smiled half-heartedly.

"Ian, have you called my daddy? He needs to know that he now has a grandson?"

Ian pretended not to hear, and instead asked how she was feeling.

"I am fine, but I need my makeup bag. I don't want visitors to see me looking like this.

I am so happy. At last, I have a son. Now everyone can stop calling me a girl making machine, and your family can now thank me for giving birth to the future heir of the Doland dynasty."

Ian was lost for words.

Later, when Donna was fully made up, Ian called her parents to give them the good news.

He remembered how his father-in-law, beaming with pride, hugged his daughter and cooed over his newborn grandson. It was as if he and Mrs King were not in the room.

He also found it hard to forget how Mr King had, in his a bullish voice, commanded the staff to give his daughter the best private room in the hospital, even though she was already in one.

He even threatened to report the midwife because, in his words, 'she was too sluggish'.

The scene made Ian cringe with disgust, but when the midwife ordered Mr King out of the room, he could not help but flash a smile at the nurse. Mrs King also seemed to have a glint of approval in her eyes.

Donna, on the other hand, did not look too impressed, but she was powerless.

Finally, someone had stood up to the mighty Mr King.

On that day Ian concluded that his father-in-law was a bully who thought his money could buy anything and anyone.

Two days later, Donna and the baby were discharged from the hospital. To say that the nurses were relieved to see the back of her was an understatement.

Ian had pleaded with her to come to London with him as, amidst other things, he had an important case the following week and he had also missed the twins, but Donna wasn't interested.

Not for the first time, she was supported by her father.

Mr King told Ian that his duty was first and foremost to his wife and son and not to the courts, conveniently leaving out the fact that he had two daughters who were just as important.

It was obvious that Donna's mother did not agree, and on this rare occasion, she voiced it.

"But Frank, Ian does have a commitment to his clients, and I think it would be good for the twins to see their brother. Donna should go to London with her husband. After all, she does have a nanny who is more than capable."

"Tessa, why do you always have to side with the others when it comes to our daughter?" Mr King retorted.

When Ian realised that the situation was fast deteriorating he decided that it was time to take matters into his hands; after all, it was his family.

"Donna, either you come with me now, or you stay with your parents, and this marriage is over. It's your choice, so choose!"

Everyone was stunned into silence.

Even Ian had thought to himself, "Where did that come from?" No one, including Donna, had heard Ian speak in that manner before.

As usual, when things were not going her way, Donna burst into tears, but this time Ian was not moved. He started packing his wife's clothes.

Donna was left with no choice; she was London bound.

That was then, but even now Donna had not changed. Coming out here to New Zealand was mainly her idea.

She had always told him that before she died, she would like to live in either New Zealand or Australia.

Ian had indulged her because he also needed a change in environment. The cold rainy English weather wasn't doing his health any good as he had arthritis.

However, his mind was now made up.

It was time to go back to England.

It was time to stop running.

The next day Sir Ian called Father O'Connor to let him know that he and Donna would be coming back to England at the end of the month.

15

Ian and Donna had raised Jennifer, Winnie and Michael in the Catholic faith, but when they got older, the children had decided to choose their own form of worship.

Jennifer and Winnie, while at University, turned to Buddhism, then to Shintoism, and by the time they graduated they were atheists.

Ian blamed himself for the family's lack of prayer focus and his children's lack of religious fervour.

He remembered how his father had consistently stressed the need for prayer at all times and told him that prayer was the key to his forebears' success.

Unfortunately, Donna was not a fan of prayer that was not offered in the church by a priest. So, there was hardly any family prayer time.

He was however pleasantly surprised when the twins met up with some of their old sixth form friends who invited them to a Business Men's Fellowship breakfast meeting in the City.

It was at one of these breakfast meetings that both Jennifer and Winnie committed their lives to Jesus and became staunch evangelicals. It was also where they met their husbands-to-be.

Michael, on the other hand still attended the Catholic Church, but he was never subservient to its tenets. He believed in a live and let live lifestyle; as long as it did not cramp his style it was alright.

Ian's parents had been good Protestants, but when he married Donna she had persuaded him to change to the Catholic faith. He had gone with it at the time because he was ready to do anything for the love of his life. However, even though he had become a practising Catholic, he still kept the family Bible that had been passed down from his grandfather.

He always loved reading the Book of Job, especially the end where God saw him through and restored his family and fortune.

These were the words he continually clung to hoping that one day, just like Job, God would restore his family which at the moment seemed to be falling apart.

16

As much as he tried, Ian could not get his son off his mind. He remembered the day Michael came home with a young girl clinging to his arm. He introduced her as Elsie Bailey.

She was the only daughter of Lord and Lady Ambrose Bailey.

Ian occasionally played golf with Lord Ambrose in the company of other colleagues, but he did not classify him as a friend.

His wife, Lady Bertha, was a fading beauty who depended on cosmetic surgery to keep age at bay. She was also one of Donna's gossiping cronies. So, naturally, Donna was thrilled that Michael and Elsie had met. In her mind, the wedding bells were already ringing.

So it came as no real surprise that three months from that day Michael and Elsie found themselves tying the knot, albeit under controversial circumstances. Elsie was pregnant!

It was one of those society weddings where both families tried to outdo each other. All he had done was sign the cheques as Donna *went to town* intent on showing the world that nothing was too much for her beloved son, and of course showing off in the process.

During the wedding preparations, and on the day, Ian saw how domineering Michael was. Elsie had little or no say in what was happening, even though it was supposed to be her special day.

Whatever Michael said, she did!

Ian also noticed the coldness between his daughters and their mother.

Jennifer and Winnie had always said they would like to do something special for their brother on his wedding day.

Instead, their mother had gone ahead and planned her son's wedding without getting them involved, and on the day she was so busy being a society madam that she didn't even notice them.

The relationship between the girls and their mother had gone downhill over the years, but Donna didn't seem to care. However, Ian knew his wife. She was a genius at disguising her feelings. He knew that deep down she wished she had a better relationship with the twins.

His relationship with his girls, on the other hand, was one to be envied.

Unlike with Michael, Ian never had a problem with his daughters. They were intelligent, well-mannered and, most of the time, obedient. Everyone spoke well of them and complimented Donna and himself for doing such an excellent job with their upbringing.

They both ended up at King's College, London and chose to study the same subject, Classical History, after which they went on to do International Law.

When they graduated, Ian had tried his best to get the girls to come and work with the family firm, but they had other plans. Thinking back, that was one of the few times they had sort of disobeyed him, but he was okay with that.

They were both beautiful, talented young ladies and he trusted them. He knew they would succeed in whatever they chose to do and succeed they did.

At times Ian thought the girls were considerate to a fault. He remembered how they both got engaged at about the same time, and how they arranged their weddings to take place on the same day at the same venue.

He had told them that they did not have to, that money was not an issue, but they insisted because they did not want to stress friends and family.

Over the years it had been a joy to watch their marriages blossom. Ian was particularly proud of his sons-in-law. They were both responsible young men with good jobs, but most importantly they loved his daughters.

Amazingly, despite their hugely successful careers they still found time to raise lovely families.

Michael, however, was a different kettle of fish. Despite studying Law with Accountancy and Finance at Durham University and graduating with first-class honours, he had refused to follow in the family tradition of staying in the family's firm.

He met a young lady, impregnated her and then had to marry her because Donna insisted that it was the only way to make things look right.

Just thinking about everything his wayward son had put them through over the years made Ian shake his head with regret.

His mind went back to the afternoon he received a call from Richard, Jennifer's husband.

17

Richard had asked if he could meet him that afternoon, making it very clear that it was urgent. So Ian suggested that they meet over coffee in the cafe down the road from his chambers.

From the tone of Richard's voice Ian knew that it was bad news, but what was it?

For some reason, his son-in-law insisted that he could not talk about it over the phone. So Ian found himself going through one of the most nerve-racking waits of his life.

Finally, some two hours later, Richard arrived at the café.

Ian was already seated in the secluded corner that he had reserved.

Richard walked over, sat down and looked straight at his father-in-law. The young man looked distraught; he was visibly shaking. Then he said a sentence that stayed with Ian until this very day:

"The next time Michael steps foot in my house I will kill him. I just wanted to let you know."

Ian was taken aback.

This was bad; worse than what he thought, but he still did not know what had happened. He finally found the courage to ask and Richard, looking down at the table, poured it all out.

He told his father-in-law about what had happened the night before. How Michael had spent the night with them because once again Elsie had kicked him out.

He told Ian how they had heard their daughter screaming in the middle of the night; how she told him that Uncle Michael had clamped his hand over her mouth to try and keep her quiet while trying to remove his trousers, and how Uncle Michael had slapped her face when she bit his hand.

"When we heard her scream Jennifer and I rushed to her room. We opened the door, and there she was curled up in the corner of the room, shaking. You could see the fear in her eyes.

I took her in my arms, tried to calm her down. I told her to tell me what happened, but all she did was shake her head and point to the door. Then Jennifer noticed the mark on her daughter's cheek and the tear in her pyjamas.

When she finally calmed down a little, she let me carry her to our bedroom. It was when Jennifer went downstairs to make her a cup of hot chocolate that little Frances opened up and told me everything."

Ian noticed that Richard was trembling; he could almost feel the rage. He placed a hand on his shoulder to comfort him. The young man shook his head as tears rolled down his cheeks.

Richard gathered himself together and went on.

"Jennifer changed Frances' pyjamas, and after drinking her hot chocolate, she fell asleep on our bed. I tried to appear relaxed for Frances' sake, but Jennifer knew I was holding something back.

When I told her what had happened, she didn't want to believe me, but we both agreed that if Frances did bite Michael's hand, the evidence would be visible."

Richard told Ian how they had knocked on the door to the guest room. They could hear the water running in the bathroom, but the door remained shut. He kept banging the door and calling out Michael's name, but there was no response. Richard was on the verge of breaking the door down when his wife advised him to wait.

"He can't stay in there forever honey. When he opens the door, we'll be here waiting."

Richard told Jennifer to stay with Frances in the bedroom, but he was going nowhere.

At about six o'clock in the morning, Richard heard the key to the guest room door turning. Jennifer, who did not get any sleep either, heard it too. They both watched as the door gradually opened, and Michael's head peeped out.

Then Michael saw Richard.

He quickly tried to shut the door, but it was too late.

Richard charged into the room and wrestled Michael to the ground.

There it was, Frances' teeth mark engraved on Michael's left hand!

Jennifer stood by the door in tears.

"You ungrateful swine. We open the doors of our house to you, and this is how you repay us. Never, ever set foot in my home again."

Ian didn't know what to say. He could hardly contain the shame he felt. He couldn't even bring himself to look Richard in the eye when he apologised for his son's treacherous behaviour.

When Richard left, Ian remembered sitting downcast at the table for a least another hour. He was going to have to tell Donna.

Ian knew she his wife would not take this well; he was right.

When he told her, she got upset because Richard had not come to her first. If anyone was going to spread ugly rumours about her son, then she wanted to be the first to know about it.

As Michael had been kicked out there was no other place for him to go but his parents' house.

Unfortunately, when he walked through the door, the first person he saw was his father. Ian confronted Michael with what

Richard had told him.

Michael denied ever going near his little niece and weaved a whole bunch of lies accusing her of having a crush on him and trying to get him into trouble. Even when Ian asked, "How does a little seven-year-old girl get to have a crush on an old man who happened to be her uncle?", Michael stood by his story, adding that he was the innocent victim of Frances' and her parents lies.

Donna did not say a word.

18

Ian's mind went back to how, after Michael's wedding, he and Donna had spent two refreshing months in their villa on the Island of Corfu.

The weather was great, and Ian enjoyed being pampered by the resident caretaker, as well as his wife. It was also a time for him to unload the many burdens he was carrying.

When they returned to England, Michael had come to see him at home and asked if he could join the family firm. It was a very pleasant surprise for Ian who had given up on his son coming on board.

For someone who did not exactly like taking instructions from anyone, including his parents, Michael appeared to be adjusting quite well to his new work environment.

Then one day, about six months later, Ian walked into his office to find Mrs Bridget Albright, who had been his secretary for more than twenty years, in tears.

Ian was horrified as to what might have happened and unconsciously found himself hoping that it had nothing to do with his son.

When he asked her what the matter was, she bluntly refused to tell him, and despite his persistence, he soon realised that he wasn't going to get a word out of her.

Later on, that day, another senior secretary, who just happened to be Ian's distant cousin, asked if she could have a word.

That was when Ian heard the full story.

In a nutshell, Michael had verbally abused Mrs Albright because she told him to take his feet off his father's table, which she deemed disrespectful.

Ian thanked her, and as she left his office asked her to tell Mrs Albright that he would like to see her.

Bridget's eyes were still puffy when she walked in. Ian told her that he had heard what happened and apologised profusely for his son's rude behaviour.

To Ian's surprise, when he promised to talk to Michael and make things right she pleaded with him not to as she could not afford to lose her job; a job she needed to take care of her disabled husband.

Ian could not understand why she thought she would be sacked, especially as she had done nothing wrong. Apart from that, he considered her to be the best secretary anyone could ever have.

Mrs Albright was loyal to the firm, and more importantly, she was loyal to him and his family. In fact, he had recently been thinking about giving her a salary raise and, even though she had not complained, employing an assistant who would help her out with her hectic work schedule.

Seeing Sir Ian's confused look she told him how Michael had said he planned to replace her with someone younger and more pleasing on the eye once he took over the firm.

Ian assured her that he had no intention of retiring or handing control over to his son anytime soon, and as Michael had no authority in the running of the firm's affairs, she had nothing to worry about.

He also seized the opportunity to tell her that he would be giving her a salary raise, and advised that she and her husband go away on a well-deserved holiday, all expenses paid.

After lunch, Ian called Michael into his office.

As usual, his son denied everything. He accused his father of always taking sides against him, and how, if it were his mother, she would never believe such a 'lie'.

Michael also told him that it was his fault that the office staff looked down on him, and how things would have been different if he had given him a senior role in the firm.

Ian was seething with anger. Even though his son's behaviour did not exactly surprise him, it was becoming increasingly irritating.

Finally, Ian could take no more. For the first time, he found himself doing something he never thought he would do.

He asked Michael's mother to come to his office!

When Donna arrived, Michael was still in Ian's office.

He told Michael to tell his mother exactly what he had accused him of. Without giving it a second thought, Michael reiterated every word to his mother. Surprisingly Donna did not agree with her son, but unsurprisingly she had a roundabout way of showing it.

She told Michael that even though she thought it was wrong of his father not to offer him a senior role with the firm, he had to abide by the rules if he was to run the company once his father retired. Then Donna asked to speak with Mrs Albright and once again, to Ian's surprise, apologised to her for her son's rudeness and insisted that Michael did likewise.

Michael had tried to wriggle out of the apology, but when he looked at his mother, he knew that he couldn't. Michael was left with no choice but to do as his mama had told him.

From that day on Michael's behaviour in the office was exemplary. Maybe knowing that his salary and allowances could be stripped away, as well as considering that he and Elsie were expecting their first child had something to do with that.

19

Exactly six months and two days after their wedding day, Michael and Elsie had their first child. A baby girl.

She looked just like Jennifer, Michael's older sister, but had Elsie's lovely green eyes. They named her Dora May.

After Dora May the couple had Michael Jr. He was a big, happy baby. He weighed ten pounds and bounced out with a smile.

Four years after Michael Jr., Elsie gave birth to their second daughter, Tricia. Tricia's birth was a stressful one for Elsie, and at some point, the doctors were afraid they would lose both of them, but miraculously they both pulled through.

Afterwards, the doctor advised Elsie and Michael that it would not be wise to have another child as the consequences could be dire.

After Tricia's birth, Elsie was not herself.

She started having nightmares, seeing herself drowning in her own blood, and just as she was about to die she would wake up.

The trauma became unbearable. Elsie started losing weight drastically and gradually retreated into her shell. It came as no real surprise when she was diagnosed with severe depression, and admitted to hospital.

Ian remembered how Elsie's parents had said that once their

daughter had been discharged, they would like her and their three grandchildren to stay with them for a while.

Michael did not seem to mind, and so for six months he commuted between his home in London, the office and the Baileys Mansion in Little Fellows, Buckinghamshire.

When Elsie and the children finally came back home, Michael decided to enrol Dora May and Michael Jr. in a private school nearby so as to make the school runs more convenient for Elsie, who was feeling a lot better but was still recovering.

Then one day, out of the blue, Michael told Elsie that he would be sending the children to boarding school. Elsie had tearfully pleaded with Michael not to do this as having the children around brought a sense of normality to her life, but her words fell on deaf ears. So, when Dora May was nine, and Michael Jr. was seven they were both whisked away to St Cyprian's School in Swindon.

The school was one of the best schools around. It admitted children between the ages of three and eighteen and the fees were astronomical. So it came as no surprise that the school only seemed to admit rich kids.

Most of Michael's friends' children attended the school, so he had decided to enrol Dora May and Michael Jr. there too. It was all about status.

He had already discussed the plan with his mother, and as long as it was good for the family name, it was alright with her. Ian, on the other hand, knew nothing about it. If he did he most likely would have objected.

On the day the children left for school, everyone cried. Everyone except Michael that is.

With the children being away Elsie's depression relapsed, but Michael was not too bothered, or maybe he just never noticed. Instead, he decided to take up part-time teaching at St Magdalene's College where he took on a senior class in what he called Classical Medieval History and Literature.

The principal of the school, Revd. Mike O'Brien who was a family friend, had welcomed Michael with open arms. The priest reckoned that what Michael had to offer would help prepare the students for whatever career they would eventually venture into.

Unfortunately, Michael had not forsaken his wild ways. With age, and being a family man, he had developed a habit of deception and manipulation that most times hid his true nature from those around him, especially his students.

Michael's lectures took place once a week, every Thursday evening at six o'clock, and they were eagerly anticipated. Most of his students enjoyed his repartee and knowledge of the ancient world. He told stories about Helen of Troy, Agamemnon, Achilles, Hector and all the Greek mythologies, and they simply loved it.

Michael would drive over to the school, and after his lecture would spend the night in his parents' country home, which was only a few miles away. Then in the morning he would drive back to London.

Elsie did not seem to mind this arrangement, but then she was not exactly in the right state of mind.

Michael had only been at St Magdalene's College for roughly five months when Josephine Kimberly, one of his students, turned sixteen.

20

Being a member of the school's Christian Fellowship, Josephine Kimberly, or Josie, as her family and friends called her, had always been passionate about telling people about Jesus.

She had lost and gained friends because she never stopped hounding them. Some had come to believe, while others simply called her a nut case and a fanatic, but she never gave up.

Josie often told Michael that the sites he mentioned in his lectures were also in the Bible and that Apostle Paul had lived and worked in quite a few of them. She always had a way of bringing the stories that Michael spoke about back to how Christianity came to be in those regions. Michael would listen and promise to continue their conversation whenever time permitted.

This went on for some time, and after a while, Michael seemed to respond positively. So, Josie decided to invite Michael to her sixteenth birthday party, where she planned to make an altar call. She had asked her parents and the College principal if it would be alright to invite him, and they said it was okay.

The Matron, Mrs Joanna Simpson, and the Chaplain Revd. Timothy Dean would be in charge of making sure that the students behaved themselves, and Josie's older brother Bruce, who had always protected her, even though he was only eighteen, would also be there. So, what could go wrong?

PART FOUR

HOME, SWEET HOME

21

Josie went straight to her room and locked the door. She sat on the floor and wept bitterly. She found it hard to take in everything that had happened to her over the last two months.

Had she really been that naive to believe that Michael Doland was actually genuine? Who knows, maybe this was what he had in mind from the very beginning. Maybe pretending to listen and look interested in what she told him was all just part of his grand master plan.

The more she thought about it, the more she cried.

Finally, Josie got up, took off her clothes and entered the bathroom. She turned on the shower and stood motionless as the warm water splashed over her body.

After a while, she stepped out of the water, wrapped herself in a towel and looked in the mirror. Her eyes were still a bit puffy, but apart from that she looked alright. She padded a little powder on her face and practised looking cheerful. She needed to get her act together as her little siblings would soon be back from school.

It wasn't going to be easy, but she had to be strong.

Josie had started noticing some changes in her body; frequently using the loo and a hunger for certain foods she could not stand normally. She planned to talk to her mum about it and now seemed like as good a time as any.

Then the front door burst open.

Josie's little sisters, ten-year-old Lois and Daphne who was eight, ran into the hallway. Both of them rushed headlong towards Josie and gave her a bear crushing hug that almost took the wind out of her.

"Wow, girls, calm down."

Josie tried to extricate herself.

"Just look at you, Daphne. You have grown so much since the last time I saw you. And you Lois, you're almost a woman. What have you girls been eating?"

"Well, you have lost a lot of weight, big sis. Are you alright?" Lois asked.

Josie sighed.

Lois had always been a deep thinker, even at her tender age. She always came up with ideas and questions that no one else thought about.

Looking at her two younger sisters and watching their boisterous nature made Josie feel old.

Angela, noticing the change in Josie's demeanour, told the girls to go upstairs and change.

Reluctantly, they trudged up the stairs.

Josie went to look for her father and found him unloading the car boot.

"Hello Dad, do you need any help?"

John smiled.

"I'm okay thank you. I stopped by the local KFC after picking up the girls from school. I thought you might want to eat something different."

"I'm not hungry dad. Apart from that, KFC isn't really my thing, but thank you anyway. By the way, do you know when Bruce is coming home?"

"Well, he called this afternoon to say that he should be back over the weekend. He would have been here earlier, but as this is his last term in the school, he had quite a bit of cleaning up to do."

Josie missed her big brother; that sparkle in his eyes, and his encouraging smile. Bruce always believed in her. He often told her that, "no matter how hard the situation, she had what it takes to make it through." He always inspired confidence in her. Whenever he was around, she felt safe. How she wished he was here now.

Bruce coming back from school soon made Josie think about her own education.

"Dad, I need to start looking for a home tutor who can help me prepare for my exams next year. What do you think?"

"We have plenty of time to think about that dear. For now, let us focus on your health."

"Okay."

Josie wasn't one to sit back and put up her feet up, and she didn't plan on starting now, but being her first day back she decided to take things easy.

On Saturday, they all drove to the station to pick Bruce up.

He emerged from the train with all his luggage.

Lois shook her head.

"Does he ever travel light?"

Josie and her mum giggled.

In the car, on the way home, Lois and Daphne teased their big brother about his scruffy hair and his unkempt beard. Daphne even went as far as pulling it.

There was joy in the air. It was mostly like this when the Kimberlys were together.

Bruce looked at Josie. Her eyes were distant, but he could see determination etched in the lines around her mouth.

When she caught him gazing at her, she squeezed his hand and flashed him a Josie smile. He was glad to see that quiet confidence;

it was his sister's trademark. It told him that she had not given up.

Bruce had been devastated by the attack, and how he had not been able to protect his sister from that monster. His parents told him that it was not his fault, but that did not lighten the weight of the burden he carried; the guilt he felt.

He had only been able to visit Josie in the hospital a few times because of his classes. Bruce didn't want to go back to school at the time. All he wanted to do was stay by his sister's side, but his mother had convinced him otherwise.

To make it to Warwick University, where he planned to study International Law, he would have to pass his final A' level examinations, which were fast approaching.

With his exams now done and dusted, he planned to be there for his sister.

At the moment Bruce was a mixed bag of emotions. Even before his father had told him, he knew that Michael Doland had attacked his sister. He had so much anger bottled up inside he was afraid of what he might do to him if their paths crossed.

Bruce also found himself asking God the "Why?" question, and where He was when his sister was being subjected to such pain.

Then there was the little issue of forgiveness. Even though it was the Christian thing to do, Bruce could not see himself forgiving this animal.

By the second week of his arrival, Bruce, his mother and father had discussed Josie's situation in depth. They planned to stand by Josie through thick and thin; it was a foregone conclusion.

Josie was grateful to her family.

She knew she could always count on them, but at the same time, she did not want anyone to pity her.

Just like his parents, Bruce respected his sister's decisions: the home tutoring, not showing any pity and all that. However, hearing her use phrases like, "What has happened has happened", and "There's no need crying over spilt milk" made him feel a bit uncomfortable.

He knew it was her way of handling it, her way of staying strong, but he couldn't help but ask himself if the reality of this situation had actually dawned on his sister.

Only time would tell.

22

As the days went by Josie gradually lost her smile.

She was always tired, and the nauseous feeling seemed unending.

There were days when it felt unbearable, days when she felt like giving up.

She had not asked for any of this, so why did she have to go through with it? Josie had told herself to get a grip, but it was hard, really hard.

For some time Josie had been harbouring the thought of what it would be like if she was not in this situation; what life would be like if she was a normal sixteen-year-old.

The home tutoring was not going as planned and to make matters worse; she looked like a balloon that was about to burst.

At times she would wake up in the morning, look out of the window and watch girls her age having fun on the way to school. Josie could see the excitement in their eyes, and how they talked to each other as they skipped happily along. Even though Josie could not hear what they were saying or what was making them laugh, just seeing them look so happy made her insides turn with envy.

"I know abortion is a sin but is there anything wrong with giving a child up for adoption?" she had asked herself.

She knew it did not exactly sound Christian-like, but right now she didn't care.

The thought had lingered, and soon she found herself regularly toying with the possibility.

"If she were to go ahead with it, how would she tell her family?" she thought.

At first, they, especially her dad, had not been too keen on her keeping the child, but over the months they had come to accept that it was what she wanted.

Thanks to her mum, the house was stacked with unisex baby clothes, and her dad had already started putting the finishing touches to the baby room. Her sisters were always rubbing her tummy and arguing over who should be the first to carry the baby.

As for Bruce; she didn't know what was on her brother's mind. With him, it was more a case of, 'as long as she was happy, he was happy'.

Josie remembered the dream she thought God had given her when she awoke from the coma. It had felt so real at the time, but now she wasn't so sure.

She had gradually thought herself out of accepting that the dream was God-given, and eventually convinced herself that it was nothing more than that: A dream! After all, she had been unconscious for close to two months. It was only natural for her head to be all over the place.

Josie's mind was made up.

She was almost eight months gone, and she knew what she had to do. She had procrastinated long enough; Josie had to tell her mum and dad.

She tried to imagine how they would take it, but no matter how she played it in her mind, it never went down well.

She had already asked for so much from them, and they had gone to great lengths to make her happy. Wouldn't this be pushing things a step too far?

Josie always looked up to her mother, and for as long as she could remember it had been her dream to be just like her: a strong, independent family woman.

The last thing she wanted was to let her down, but it seemed that was about to happen.

Josie whispered to herself as she lay on her bed:

"Tomorrow, after family prayers, I'm going to tell them."

John and Angela were woken up by the sound of Josie screaming. They jumped up and ran to her room.

Josie tossed and turned, clutching her tummy.

She was shivering, even though her temperature had gone through the roof, and she was soaked in her own sweat.

Then John noticed that she was bleeding and immediately called an ambulance.

Within fifteen minutes the paramedics arrived, and for the second time in less than a year, Josie was being rushed to the hospital.

Josie slipped in and out of consciousness as the paramedics wheeled her to the emergency room.

While being examined Josie began to convulse; her body jerked, and her face paled. The medical team decided that an immediate caesarian section was needed to save both mother and the baby.

John and Angela had driven behind the ambulance and waited anxiously for several hours to hear from one of the medical staff.

Finally, a nurse approached the couple. She explained what had happened, and how it had become necessary to perform an emergency caesarian section to save both Josie and the baby.

The good news was that the operation was successful. Both mother and the baby were in a stable condition and had been moved to a private recovery room.

Despite the assurance from the nurse, John and Angela both felt a strange sense of déjà vu.

The midwife could see the look in their eyes.

She smiled.

"You can come through and see her if you want."

Josie was sound asleep when Angela walked into the room.

The only visible sign of life was the heart monitor.

The midwife checked Josie's vital signs, turned to Angela and said, "She's doing fine Mrs Kimberly," as if to put her heart at rest.

Not long after, another nurse walked into the room holding a tiny bundle wrapped in a pink blanket. She placed the little one in Mrs Kimberly's arms.

"Congratulations."

Angela smiled, tears in her eyes as she looked down at the tiny bundle of joy. With her mother's gorgeous dark blue eyes, she looked so beautiful.

"Thank You."

Over the past few months, both John and she had wondered what this moment would be like, considering how the little one had been conceived.

They loved their daughter unconditionally, but would they be able to love this baby the same way? Would they be able to accept it as part of their family?

Only time would tell, and that time had come.

Still staring at her granddaughter, Angela felt love and compassion that she had not felt in some time.

The unspoken resentment that she had harboured towards the child seemed to fade away instantly.

As Angela gently rocked the little one, she sneaked a peek at her daughter.

Josie lay on the bed, oblivious to everything going on around her. She looked so happy, so peaceful, albeit she was asleep.

It had been a while since she had seen Josie look stress-free; without a care in the world.

Her mind went back to everything her daughter had been through over the last year.

It had been tough, but Josie had taken it all in her stride. Though it had not all been plain sailing, their daughter's determination had shone through.

Now it was time for her to be strong for Josie, and her granddaughter.

The midwife took the baby from Mrs Kimberly, cleaned her and laid her in the small cot beside Josie's bed.

Josie had tossed and turned a little, but she was in no hurry to wake up.

John knocked, and quietly walked into the room.

He had been speaking to the consultant on call, and from the smile on his face, it had gone well.

"So, what did the doctor have to say?" Angela asked.

"Nothing really. Just that Josie will have to stay here a little longer because of the operation. Apart from that, both mother and baby are doing just fine."

Angela sighed with relief.

John looked at his daughter curled up on the bed.

"So… how is she?"

"Well, she hasn't woken up since I've been in the room, but I think she is fine."

"And… the baby?" John mumbled.

"She's gorgeous John. Would you like to hold her?"

John hesitated for a split second, then carried her out of his wife's arms.

He looked at the little one and smiled.

"She's beautiful!" he whispered as his eyes welled up.

23

No one said a word as the Kimberlys walked to the hospital car park.

Both Angela and John had replayed the last fortnight back in their minds over and over again and they still found it hard to believe.

Two weeks ago their Josie had experienced a death-defying delivery, but here they were, about to drive home without the baby.

Angela had noticed that when Josie woke up, she didn't look or even ask for her child.

At the time she thought her daughter was overwhelmed by the trauma she had been through, which was understandable.

It turned out she was wrong.

With her back turned to her mum and dad and the baby's cot, Josie told her parents that there was something she needed to tell them.

John and Angela looked at each other and wondered why Josie had turned away.

Angela walked over to the other side of the bed.

"What's the matter, honey?"

That's when Josie landed the bombshell.

Josie told her parents that she had changed her mind about keeping the baby; that she was not ready to be a mother, and if possible could they make plans with the hospital to have the baby adopted.

Angela was shocked. She could not believe what she just heard. She looked around and sat down.

John advised Josie not to rush into making a rash decision, and think it through.

That is when Josie told them that she had done all the thinking she needed to do over the last four months, but she just didn't know how to tell them, especially after everything they had done for her.

Angela could not understand. Josie had been adamant about keeping this baby, and now suddenly, out of the blue, she wanted to give her up.

"Why Josie, why?"

"I am sorry to disappoint you mum, but I can't do this. I just can't!"

Initially, John wasn't keen on keeping the child, but over the months he had come to accept it and was actually looking forward to the new addition to the family.

He had almost completed the baby room and the night before Josie was admitted he had set up the baby's cot. It was meant to be a surprise.

If only he had known.

He remembered how Josie had told them that she could not keep the baby, and how she planned to give it up for adoption immediately.

He recalled how his wife Angela had slumped into a chair, lost for words. He also remembered asking Josie to sleep on it, and not rush into making a decision, but he knew his daughter. Her mind was already made up.

John had left Angela and Josie in the room with the intention of going to see the doctor but instead found himself pacing up and down the hospital corridor, confused.

"Who was he supposed to tell about this situation, and what exactly was he meant to say?"

He decided not to tell anyone and instead hoped against hope that Josie would come to her senses after a good night's sleep.

He was wrong!

Angela had stayed awake most of the night.

She watched as her daughter barked at the confused nurse to take the baby away.

Angela followed the midwife, apologised for her daughter's behaviour and explained to her what was going on.

The midwife advised that they should let Josie sleep on it; that most likely she would feel a lot better when she wakes up, and therefore be able to think straight.

She was wrong!

The next day, as Angela and John spoke to Josie, she appeared even more sure that this was the right thing to.

They tried to reason with her, but their words fell on deaf ears, and when Angela suggested that she would look after the baby Josie disagreed vehemently like a girl possessed.

"Mum, this baby cannot be a part of this family."

Angela stomped out of the room. John ran after her.

"John, what has come over our daughter?"

"I wish I knew darling. What I do know is that she has had a lot of time to think about this, and it is not going to be easy to change her mind."

"So, she doesn't want to keep the baby, and she doesn't want us to look after her. What are we meant to do then?"

There had been no contact between the Kimberlys and the Dolands since they found out that Michael was the one who raped

Josie, but when Donna heard that Josie had given birth she was determined to see her grandchild.

Donna turned to Ian.

"I think it is only right for all of Michael's children to grow up under the same roof,"

"Woman, do you have no shame; not an ounce of dignity?"

Ian was angry.

"We have inflicted pain and shame on this young girl, and her family. We have not helped them in any way, yet all you can think about is how this newborn baby can be brought up under the roof of our irresponsible son."

Ian shook his head in amazement.

His wife was quick to criticise the wayward ways of other people's children, but Michael could do no wrong.

It dawned on him that Donna had turned into an amoral person; someone who had no compassion or love for others unless she had something to gain.

"I would strongly advise that you stay away from the Kimberlys. I think we have done enough damage."

Donna was used to having her way, and when she had her eyes set on something it was hard to stop her.

She looked at her husband as if to say, "Are you going to stop me?" then turned and walked away.

Right then Ian knew she would be paying the Kimberlys a visit.

Donna, in typical fashion, had bullied her way through to the hospital's private wing, and without knocking, walked straight into Josie's room. Both Angela and Josie were taken by surprise.

Her nose in the air, Donna tried to introduce herself, but Angela cut her short.

"I know who you are. What gives you the audacity to walk in here uninvited?"

"Well, I have come to see my latest grandson. I assume it is a boy?"

"Wrong, she's a girl, and by the way, can we take this outside?"

With everything that was going on, a scene with this woman in front of Josie was the last thing she needed. Angela opened the door and ushered Mrs Doland out.

When they were a safe distance from the room, Angela turned to Donna.

"What are you doing here Mrs Doland?"

"Like I said, I came to see my grandchild. Personally, I believe that Michael's daughter should be brought up with the rest of his children; under his roof. That aside, don't you think your little girl deserves to continue her education and grow up like a normal sixteen-year-old; without any excess baggage?

Well, I thought that I might be able to help. What about if I offered to carry the burden of bringing up this baby?"

Angela was finding it hard to control her anger.

"Who do you think you are? You strut in here wagging your tongue around; no remorse, not even an apology for the hell your son put my daughter through. Do you think being the mother of the brute, who unfortunately happens to be the father of this lovely baby girl gives you the right to barge in here uninvited?"

Angela turned to walk away, then stopped. She had a bit more to say.

"And by the way, bringing up this bundle of joy will not be a burden but a blessing. The only burden in our hearts right now is your beast of a son."

Lady Donna, red in the face with embarrassment, stuttered. "There…there… there is no need to use that tone, Mrs Kimberly. What I suggested is for the good of everyone concerned. Would you prefer that your daughter to be ridiculed by those around her when they find out that she is a single, teenage mum?"

Just then John Kimberly and the doctor came running along the corridor. The altercation had been brought to their attention while they were discussing Josie's situation.

Both of them looked surprised to see Lady Donna.

John hugged his wife, who was still fuming, and asked Mrs Doland what she was doing in the hospital.

Donna had regained her composure.

"Your wife will tell you what we have discussed, but I can assure you that you will be hearing from my lawyer very soon."

She turned and left the room with a flounce.

"What was that all about?" John asked, looking straight into his wife's eyes.

The doctor, realising that the couple needed a moment, went to check on Josie.

John was slightly agitated.

"So, are you going to tell me what that woman was doing here?"

"The honest truth is, I don't know. She just barged into Josie's room, without knocking, and started rambling. She didn't even know that the baby was a girl.

Luckily I was able to get her out of the room before her words did any damage."

John's curiosity was eating away at him.

"So, what did she say?"

"Well, it looks like the Dolands have plans for this child that we don't know anything about. If I heard her correctly, she seems to think that this little baby should live under the same roof as that brute because he happens to be her father. Can you imagine that?!

John, that woman is just so arrogant. Her lack of sensitivity and compassion is insufferable."

"I know what you mean. It is so unfortunate that her husband is one of the kindest human beings I have ever met. How he ended up marrying her beats me.

Anyway, for now, we need to focus on Josie and the baby. Has she changed her mind?"

"I don't know John. I hate to say this, but I think you're right. Josie seems to have made up her mind. She hasn't so much as looked at the baby, not to talk of feed, bath or even carry her.

The midwife seemed rather concerned and advised that we may need to seek help."

John sighed.

"Well, I had a word with the doctor too, and he was quite surprised. He was also concerned about what had brought about the sudden change of heart and advised that we give Josie some time to think it through. However, if she still intends to go ahead, then we will have to call in Child Services.

But don't let us give up just yet darling. Let us give her a few more days before we broach the subject again. Hopefully, by then she will see things in a different light."

24

It had been six days since the birth of Josie's baby girl.

The Kimberlys had just finished speaking to the charge nurse, and even though there still had been no contact between mother and baby, things seemed to be looking up.

John knocked on Josie's door, and they both walked in.
Just like the nurse had said, there was something almost beatific in her countenance. She even greeted them with a smile.
John and Angela looked at each other; was this an answer to prayer?

"Good morning mum, good morning dad."
Josie paused.
"Remember you told me to give this issue some thought before making a decision? Well, I have."
John and Angela looked at their daughter with an expectant silence. Was this the moment they had been hoping for?
"I have thought long and hard for the last four months about this situation, and even though I know you think I am just a child, coming to this decision hasn't been easy for me at all. I..., we cannot keep this baby!"

Head stooped, Angela sighed.

John tried to hide his disappointment, and asked his daughter what had made her change her mind so drastically?

Her words left him broken.

"Dad, each time I think about this baby I find myself reliving that night; the brutal and violent abuse I suffered at the hands of someone I had started to trust.

At times the thoughts fill me with fear, sometimes shame, but most times they leave me angry.

There hasn't been one day that thinking about this child has brought a smile to my face, not a day that it has made me leap for joy.

I thought that having the baby and holding her in my arms would change everything, but I was wrong. It has only made things worse.

I can't even bring myself to look at her, let alone carry her."

Josie, who had appeared rather chirpy minutes earlier was now a tearful mess.

"Dad, it hurts so much. What kind of a mother chooses to abandon her child? I feel so terrible inside, but how can I bring her up when each time I see her, or even think about her, all I feel is fear, shame, hatred and anger?

It is not fair on the little one. She deserves so much more than that. After all, she has done nothing wrong, so why should she suffer the consequences?"

John walked over to his daughter's bedside and wrapped her in a warm embrace.

It dawned on him how they had taken this situation for granted.

Josie was only a child; sixteen years old, but still only a child. Yet they had unconsciously allowed her to carry this burden almost all alone.

John whispered in her ear.

"We're so sorry Josie."

It had been fifteen minutes since the lady from Child Services had left the room, but John, Angela and Josie still sat quietly pondering what she had said.

The woman had taken the time to explain to the Kimberlys the implications of giving up a child. None of it sounded pleasant, but the part about the baby having to stay in a foster home until they found a family suitable to adopt her was hard to bear.

Finally, Josie broke the silence.

"Does she really have to go to a foster home? There has got to be another way."

John looked at his wife. She shook her head. She knew what was going through his mind.

"Josie, please excuse your mum and me for a few minutes."

Josie's parents got up and walked out of the room.

As they stood outside the reception doors, John tried to get his wife to understand his point of view.

Angela did not agree.

"Look, I know that Michael is the child's father and all that, but do you really think bringing up a child, our granddaughter, anywhere near that man is a good idea?"

"Angela, I know it's not ideal, and trust me, Michael will get what's coming to him, but I do think it is better than her staying in a foster home before finally being adopted by an unknown family who we can only hope will actually love her.

At least we know the Dolands. If we do agree for them to look after our granddaughter, it will be with an assurance of free, unhindered access.

None of Josie's rights as the child's mother will be relinquished. So, if somewhere along the way she does change her mind, she'll be able to see her daughter whenever she wants."

Angela hissed.

"But that Doland woman; she does my head in. I can't bear the thought of her getting her way again."

"I know darling, but we need to focus on what's best for Josie and her daughter. Don't worry, I will deal with the Dolands."

Josie was asleep when her parents came back to the room. Angela tapped her daughter and woke her up.

"Josie dear, your father and I have something we want to tell you."

For the next thirty minutes, Angela told Josie everything she and her father had discussed.

It took some convincing from both her parents, but finally, Josie agreed that it might be the best thing to do under the circumstances.

"So, tomorrow I will call Sir Ian and talk things over with him. At least I know I can take him at his word," John said.

Early the next morning John was on the phone with Sir Ian.

Sir Ian apologised for everything his family had put the Kimberlys through, and that even though he knew there was nothing he could do to take the pain away, he would do everything within his ability to make sure that Josie's daughter was given the life she deserves.

He thanked John again for allowing him and his family to be a part of their granddaughter's life, and in confidence advised John that it would be a wise idea if they drew up a contract of some kind to seal everything they had spoken about, especially concerning Josie's access rights to her daughter.

Even though he didn't say it, John knew this was mainly because Sir Ian did not trust his wife and his son.

There was one last thing that John had asked of Sir Ian, and even though it was no easy task, Mr Doland had given his word.

Angela and Josie were shocked when John told them what he had asked Sir Ian to do.

Josie was hesitant, and understandably so.

Angela, after giving it some thought, decided to take it with a pinch of salt. Going by what her husband had told her, Sir Ian was a good man, but getting him to do this was a bridge too far.

It was never going to happen.

John met Donna and her son in the private ward reception.

Michael cowered behind his mother. He could not bring himself to look Mr Kimberly in the eye, but that didn't bother John. He had his gaze fixed solely on the monster that had tried to mess up his daughter's life.

John had often wondered what he would have done to Michael if he was not a God fearing man. Even now, just looking at the Doland boy made him angry.

"Could he ever forgive him?" John wondered.

He wasn't sure he could.

Mrs Doland was unusually well-mannered, greeting Mr Kimberly with a polite smile and explaining the purpose of their visit.

She obviously did not know that John was behind it all.

"Michael has come to see Josie. He has come to apologise."

It was easy to see that the words were heavy on Donna's lips. She wasn't used to being in this situation.

"Well, I doubt he'll be able to do that, but I sure would like to hear him try."

John's voice trembled as it got louder.

"By the way, is there any particular reason why you are acting as your son's mouthpiece Mrs Doland? I would have thought that a man who didn't have a problem raping an innocent, helpless girl would at least have the courage to speak up for himself."

Michael, his chin still stuck to his chest, whispered,

"I'm sorry Mr Kimberly. I made a terrible mistake. I was drunk. I didn't know what I was doing. I…"

John raised his hand to shut him up.

"Do not apologise to me, young man. Do you remember the

girl whose life you almost destroyed? Well, it's her forgiveness you need, not mine."

John turned to Mrs Doland.

"And after the appalling behaviour you displayed the other day, I believe you also owe my wife an apology."

Donna stuttered.

"Yes, I… I believe I do."

John walked Donna and the Doland boy into Josie's room.

Angela still could not believe what had happened. Donna Doland had actually taken a huge slice of humble pie and said, 'Sorry'.

She had rambled on about not knowing what came over her, speaking without thinking and hoping that the mild altercation would not damage their relationship, which was weird considering they didn't have one.

While her mum was still lost in disbelief, Josie sat on the edge of her bed and replayed Michael's apology. Not once had she looked at him while he spoke; it was hard enough being in the same room as him.

He had gone on and on about how sorry he was and how he appreciated all she had done for him.

He said all the right things, but deep down inside she doubted if he would ever change.

The only time she spoke was when Michael and his mother were about to leave the room.

"Michael, make sure you look after her."

On the morning of the day Josie was to be discharged, Michael's wife, along with his mother, came to pick up Josie's daughter.

All the necessary paperwork which John and Sir Ian agreed to put in place had been taken care of the day before.

Now baby Josie was off to live with the Dolands.

After Lady Donna and Elsie had left with the child, Josie burst into tears.

John and Angela tried to console her, but their daughter was inconsolable.

Josie was starting to regret that she never held her, never fed her, never bathed her and never even looked at her.

What kind of a mother does that to her child?

Was she really that heartless?

Later on that afternoon, the doctor popped in to examine Josie one last time before discharging her.

He smiled at Josie.

"You are one lucky young lady, I can tell you that."

Josie smiled, but she didn't feel that lucky.

As they drove through the hospital gates, Josie felt an emptiness inside. The more she pondered what had happened over the last fortnight, the more it dawned on her that she may have made a terrible mistake.

From the moment she stepped out of the hospital John had noticed a confused, bewildered look in his daughter's eyes.

He could only imagine what was going through her mind.

John knew she was a tough young lady but what she had been through over the last nine months was enough to break anyone.

The drive home was unusually, but unsurprisingly quiet. Angela had her gaze fixed on the road ahead, and each time John looked in his rear view mirror he saw Josie peering through the side window.

John was about to break the silence when he heard Josie's voice; it was just above a whisper.

"Will I ever see my daughter again?"

There was a slight pause. Angela and John looked at each other for a split second.

"Whenever you want to honey, whenever you want to," John replied.

No one uttered another word until they got home.

The house was empty. Bruce was still on campus, and Josie's

little sisters were not back from school.

Angela took her daughter's hand and led her into the living room while her father brought in Josie's holdall.

As her mother made her comfortable on the sofa, Josie hugged her and kissed her on the cheek.

"I love you so much mum, and I want to thank you for everything you've done for me; both you and dad. I am so sorry for everything I have put you through."

"That's okay. Let me get you something to drink. Would you like a mug of hot chocolate?"

"That would be lovely. Thanks, mum."

Angela tried to fight back the tears as she placed the hot chocolate, along with some home-made cookies, on the stool beside her daughter.

Josie thanked her mum. Then she ate all the cookies, finished her drink, lay her head on Angela's lap and slept.

Angela spent some time stroking Josie's hair and just looking at her little, grown up daughter.

"Lord, please help Josie through this."

Leaving Josie asleep on the sofa, Angela busied herself with tidying Josie's room and getting lunch ready for Lois and Daphne, who would soon be back from school.

She was so engrossed in what she was doing that she hadn't given any thought to what they would tell the girls when they realised that the baby they had looked forward to seeing for so long wasn't here.

The moment she dreaded soon came when the girls, as usual, burst into the living room chorusing,

"Where is our baby, our little baby niece?"

They jumped on their big sister, who was now awake thanks to their noisy entrance and demanded to see the newest member of the family.

When Josie was not forthcoming, they took matters into their own hands and ran upstairs.

As expected, Lois and Daphne came down wearing forlorn looks of disappointment.

"Where is she?" they asked.

"Come on girls, you can see that your sister is tired. Why don't you go and freshen up; change out of your uniforms, thank God for seeing you through another school day, and let us have dinner."

For a moment the girls stood defiantly, looking at Josie, waiting for a response, but their big sister said nothing.

Disappointed, they trudged upstairs.

A damper had been placed on their excitement.

Josie didn't know what to tell her little sisters.

It just seemed a bit too complicated for them to understand.

"Mum, what do I tell the girls?"

"Well, we might have to tell them that she's spending some time with her other family."

It wasn't exactly the truth, but for now, it was all they could come up with.

25

The Kimberlys were a closely-knit family, and they did most things together. So, it felt a bit awkward not telling the girls what actually happened to their baby niece, and with Bruce coming home soon, both John and Angela wondered how they would break the news to him.

When Bruce arrived, he noticed that Josie was no longer pregnant. Strangely no one had said anything about what happened, so he decided not to broach the topic.

It was Saturday morning. Three days had gone by, and the silence was killing him. Bruce could take no more. He went downstairs, knocked, and walked into his father's study.
He knew he would be in there.

"Dad, what is going on? I have been home for three days, and no one has said a word about Josie's baby. I have had to tread on eggshells trying not to say or do the wrong things but I can't do that anymore. I need to know the truth.
What happened to the baby?"

John saw the look in Bruce's eyes. He knew he could no longer hide the truth from the young man.

"Sit down son. I'll start by saying that there was nothing wrong with the baby. It was a traumatic delivery. Your sister had to undergo an emergency caesarian section, but both she and the baby made it through okay. Thank God for that."

"So where is the baby then?"

"Patience son. You see, when your sister woke up after the operation she told the midwife that she did not want the baby in the same room as her.
Initially, when your mother heard she thought Josie was overwhelmed by the trauma she had been through, but it turned out that wasn't the case.
Apparently, after giving it a lot of thought, which we were unaware of at the time, Josie had decided she could not keep the baby, and neither could we."

Bruce looked confused. John took a deep breath.

"When she finally told us, I advised her not to rush into anything and asked her to take her time to think it through.
Your mum and I were rather surprised and disappointed, but what could we do. We prayed that she would see things differently as time went by, but... you know your sister.
It had taken her four long months to make this decision.
Her mind was already set."

Bruce still had a puzzled look on his face, wondering where all this was leading to.

"Anyway, your sister's plan was to give the baby up for adoption. However, after listening to the unpleasant things that the lady from Child Services had to say, we all knew that adoption was not an option.

After much deliberation, your mother and I came up with an alternative. It was hard, but we believe it was the lesser of two evils."

"And what was this alternative?"

John hesitated then he mumbled.
"The Dolands."
Bruce's jaw dropped.
"The Dolands! You mean after all the pain and shame they have brought upon Josie and our family you still thought it was okay to entrust them with this little child?"
Bruce could not believe his ears.
The disgust and unpleasant surprise were evident in his tone.
"Dad, how could you?"
John was lost for words. He knew his son was hurting, and he had every right to feel this way, but what could he say.
"And Josie actually agreed to this?"

At that point Josie and her mother walked into the room; standing outside listening to the conversation, they couldn't bear it any longer.

Bruce looked at his sister; he could see the answer to his question written on her face.

"Josie, what happened? I thought you wanted to keep the baby?"
"I do... I did, but..."
The tears streamed down her cheeks.
"I tried to be strong, I really did, but..."

Angela wrapped her daughter in her arms and looked at her son. "Bruce, this was not a decision made lightly. The last few months have been a struggle for your sister, to say the least.
Your father and I just wished she had told us about it sooner

so we could have helped her through it all. Anyway, that's all water under the bridge now.

Considering what happened with Michael, and knowing the heartless character that Lady Donna is, the Dolands would be the last family that we would give the little baby to, but Sir Ian gave his word that he would look after her.

He also promised to ensure that your sister's right to see her daughter whenever and wherever she wants would not be diminished in any way.

Josie is the little one's mother, and that is never going to change."

Bruce was not convinced.

"And what makes this Sir Ian any different from his wife and son? How do we know that they are not birds of a feather; cut from the same cloth?"

"The truth is, we don't. However, we know that Sir Ian is a good man; a man of integrity. Your father trusts him, and therefore so do I."

Bruce looked away.

Josie looked at her parents.

"Mum, dad, can I please speak to Bruce alone?"

John and Angela left the room and closed the door behind them.

Angela, John and the girls had just finished breakfast when they heard the study door open.

A few seconds later Josie and Bruce walked out smiling at each other.

Lois and Daphne jumped out of their chairs and flew into their arms, almost pushing both of them to the floor.

Bruce chuckled.

"You girls have put on some weight."

Angela turned to Josie and Bruce, curiosity in her eyes. "Are you okay?"

They looked at each other, smiled, and nodded.

26

Josie had always found it easy to speak to her big brother, but the last three days had been very challenging. Finally being able to talk to Bruce had given her a chance to release pent-up emotions.

Josie reminisced.

"Good old Bruce, always playing the big brother.
She thought back on their escapades and wondered what she would have done without him.

While they were in the study, Josie told Bruce all that had happened, but for some reason, she didn't say what she planned to do next.
She wanted to, she really did, but deep down she knew that Bruce would not understand, and therefore would not approve of her plan.

As she lay in bed that night, Josie thought about how to contact her aunt Jacqueline, her mother's younger sister who lived in Scotland.
Even though she was a bit confused about what to do, the one thing she was sure of was that she needed to spend some

time away from home, and at the moment staying with Auntie Jacqueline seemed like the most viable option.

She tossed and turned as she contemplated telling Bruce about her plan to leave home. She really wanted to tell him, but she knew that he would try and talk her out of it, and he would definitely tell mum and dad.

Then, out of nowhere, she remembered the night of her sixteenth birthday.

Josie could see the look in Michael's eyes, she could smell the strong, foul stench of alcohol on his breath, and even hear herself crying, but then she saw her beautiful baby girl.

It was strange considering she didn't know what her daughter looked like, but Josie had no doubt that she was an angel.

In her mind she tried not to link the innocent baby to the brute that raped her; she tried, but to no avail.

Josie buried her tear-laden face in her pillow.

"Dear God, please help me."

She could say no more.

Josie felt a lot better when she opened her eyes later that morning, even though the thought of running away lurked in the back of her mind.

She jumped up, had a bath and slipped into her church clothes.

Secretly she hoped that God would back up her plan and speak to her heart during the service, but she doubted it.

Most likely He didn't approve either.

The drive to church was refreshing.

The Kimberly clan were all together again; Lois and Daphne singing away, mum and Josie clapping along, dad bobbing his head up and down and Bruce acting all macho before bursting into laughter when the girls started tickling him.

Josie had always enjoyed being in church and today was no

exception.

The songs were uplifting, and Pastor Daniel's message was interesting, to say the least.

He spoke about God being Omniscient; having infinite knowledge and understanding at all times.

How nothing caught him unawares, and how only He knew the end from the beginning and the beginning from the end.

As the pastor preached, Josie's mind replayed everything that had happened over the last ten months.

Josie knew that God's ways were not the same as hers and that there was always a purpose behind His grand master plan, but did she really have to endure this hurt, this pain?

It was a question that she had tried to ignore even though it always seemed to plague her mind, but listening to the message from the pulpit brought it to the fore again.

After the service Josie noticed a few congregants stealing glances at her. It didn't take a magician to know what was going through their minds, but Josie wasn't really bothered.

She was just happy that, even though many church members had gone out of their way to say hello, no one had asked her any prying questions.

As they walked to the car park, Josie looked back to see where mum and dad were.

At first, she couldn't see them, then she spotted them talking to Pastor Daniel.

When she looked back, her eyes met Bruce's.

He smiled.

"Don't worry Josie, it might not be easy, but everything is going to be alright."

"Thanks, Bruce."

Josie looked away, the guilt she felt made it hard to look her brother in the eye.

"Home, sweet home!"

Lois screamed happily as she burst through the front door.

There really is no place like home, Josie thought, but she needed to get away from these familiar surroundings that kept bringing back memories of her recent past.

Josie looked on and smiled as they all relaxed in the living room. They joked, they pulled each other's legs, and the girls tickled Bruce to tears.

Josie was struggling to fight back the tears.

She thought to herself, "I am really going to miss all this."

Then she got up and made her way to the bathroom.

There was a knock on the bathroom door.

"Are you okay Josie?"

It was her mum.

"I'm fine mum."

Josie must have spent close to twenty minutes just gazing at herself in the mirror, thinking about all she was going to leave behind, and the uncertain future that lay ahead.

"Dinner is almost ready."

"I'll be done soon. Thank you, mum."

After dinner, and sharing a prayer together, Daphne and Lois kissed their mum, dad and Josie good night while Bruce, who had been roped into telling them a bedtime story, followed the girls upstairs.

John and Angela both looked exhausted, and before too long they dozed off, hand in hand, on the couch.

Josie watched as her parents slept.

The last couple of weeks had been a real roller coaster for them; she had put them through so much.

The last thing she wanted to do was cause them any more pain, but it was looking inevitable.

Finally, Josie woke her parents and kissed them both good night.

"I love you both so much."

"We love you too honey."

John and Angela wrapped their arms around their daughter and gave her a long hug, then they all went upstairs to sleep.

27

Things were getting back to normal in the Kimberly household, but Bruce still had unfinished business with his father.

There was still something bothering him, something he couldn't quite understand.

He knew he would find the answers in his dad's study, so he made his way downstairs.

"Hi Dad, can we talk?"

As he looked at his son, he knew it was going to be another tough conversation.

"Yeah sure, what's on your mind, Bruce?"

"You know, before Josie told me what happened, I was sure that you and mum had given the baby to the Dolands to sort of keep up appearances, and to maintain a good Christian image, but I was wrong, and I want to apologise for that."

John smiled and gave his son a pat on the back.

"That's alright Bruce. I guess if I was in your shoes I might have felt the same way too."

Bruce continued.

"But there is still something I don't quite understand."

"And what might that be?"

"After being confirmed as the one who assaulted my sister, why didn't you persuade Josie to press charges against Michael Doland?

I have sat down and tried to replay the whole situation in my head. I know that, even though mum encouraged her to, Josie was reluctant to give a statement, and insisted that she did not want to press charges.

I know she said we should 'leave it all in God's hands' and stuff, but you didn't even try and persuade her. It was as if you didn't want her to in the first place.

I remember being very disgruntled at the time. None of it made any sense to me. I mean, what kind of a father sits back and watches his daughter go through such a traumatic experience, and does nothing about it?"

There was a brief silence.

All the while Bruce had dropped his head, unable to meet his father's gaze, but now he looked up.

"I know you dad; you're not that kind of a father. So, what was it? Why didn't you fight for Josie?"

John turned and backed his son.

"Bruce, trust me, I would die for anyone of you, but there is a lot more to this, and I am not sure you will understand."

"Dad, I'm not Lois or Daphne, or even Josie. I know I am your son, but I am also a grown man. Rather than assume that I won't understand, why don't you just tell me."

John Kimberly could hear a firm determination in the tone of his son's voice.

Like a dog with a bone, he knew Bruce was not going to let this go.

"Sit down Bruce."

Bruce took a seat.

"I am about to tell you a secret that I have kept bottled up for years. By the time I finish you will either applaud me for being appreciative of the good done for my family and me or disdain me for being cowardly and weak."

John heard his son gulp.

"My parents, your grandparents came to this country as refugees during the Second World War.
Despite hearing about the atrocities going on in Poland at the time, most of the authorities over here turned a deaf ear.
Your grandparents were young and very academic. They were well known in their native Poland, but because my mother was a Jew, my father decided that they had to find a way to flee the country.

They didn't know anyone when they arrived here. Father could speak and understand a little English, but mother couldn't, so communication wasn't exactly straightforward.
On the day they went for accreditation at the Office of Displaced Persons (New Arrivals) they were accused of being German spies.
Despite their authentic paperwork and all the evidence they provided, the British authorities threw them in prison indefinitely."

Bruce was getting impatient, and couldn't see the relevance of the story.

"Dad, what has this got to do with what happened to Josie?"

John flashed his son a stern look and continued.

"You can imagine the fear and frustration this young couple went through, yet they refused to despair.
My father felt that being alive in a cell in England was still better than the torture they would have been put through in their native Poland."

There was a knock on the door. It was Angela bringing in her husband's morning tea.

"Thank you, darling."

Angela left the room and closed the door behind her.
John took a sip of his tea and carried on.

"While still incarcerated, a British Aristocrat who happened to be a lawyer affiliated with the Office of Displaced Persons decided to listen to what this young Koniecpol couple had to say.
For some reason, he believed they were not German spies, and they had been imprisoned unlawfully. Then just when the British authorities were about to sentence my parents to a certain death by sending them back to Poland, this gentleman stood in and took it upon himself to argue on their behalf.
He stood surety for my parents.

When my parents were released and had nowhere to go, this same gentleman invited them into his home.
They lived with him for more than six months while they tried to find a place of their own. He fed them, and gave them shelter, wanting nothing in return.
It goes without saying that they became very close friends, and remained so till the day they died.

"So, this British gentleman who rescued your parents, who was he?"
"Well, that British lawyer was Sir Ian Doland's father, and like I told your mother before we got married, if not for him I most likely wouldn't be here."

Bruce sighed.

He could see his father's point, but was that really enough to let Michael Doland get off scot-free?

Somehow, Bruce didn't think so.

John could see the discontented expression on his son's face.

"Bruce, I know it might not make that much sense to you at the moment, but that is my reason, and if I have let you down I am sorry.

My so-called sitting back and doing nothing attitude had nothing to do with being weak. I detest what Michael Doland did to my daughter. There is not a day that goes by that I don't think about it.

To be honest, I am struggling to find space in my heart to forgive that boy.

The one thing I know is that no one does a thing like that and gets away with it.

Michael Doland will pay for his crimes one day."

John broke down in tears.

28

It had just gone past three in the morning on the last day of July.

Josie got to her feet and packed a few clothes, and other necessities into her holdall.

She brushed her teeth, had a shower, dressed up, and waited for the break of dawn.

At the first glimpse of daylight, Josie picked up her holdall, slowly opened her door, and crept down the carpet-cushioned steps.

Then she quietly unlocked the front door, and stood in the doorway.

As she looked out onto the streets, happy thoughts flashed through her mind, and then she remembered Bruce, again.

She felt bad leaving without confiding in him, but it was better this way.

Josie closed the door and walked to the bus stop.

The night before Josie had called her best friend, Lily Ann Burton, and told her what she planned to do. She also told Lily

Ann that she was going to need her help.

Lily Ann had agreed to help her friend but made Josie promise that when she came over to hers, she would have to tell her why she was running away.

Josie got off the bus and walked towards her friend's place.

As she approached the house, she saw Lily Ann waiting by the gate.

Lily Ann quietly smuggled Josie into her bedroom, making sure they didn't wake her parents or her brother.

Apart from being best friends, Lily Ann and Josie shared a striking resemblance. Seeing them together, one would think they were actually identical twins.

They met in their first year at St Magdalene's College and had since become inseparable. Unsurprisingly they were also roommates.

It was Lily Ann who ran to the matron's office to report that Josie was missing the morning after her sixteenth birthday.

She still blamed herself for not sleeping in the room that night.

"So Josie, why are you running away? I can understand why you might not want to tell your parents, but Bruce. Why didn't you tell Bruce? You know how much he cares for you. This is really going to hurt him."

"Lily, I know you might find it hard to understand, but I need to get away. After everything that has happened, I need to be somewhere that won't remind me of the pain.

I really wanted to tell Bruce, but he would have tried to talk me out of it.

I just think it is better this way."

"Oh well, your secret is safe with me, but I'm sure you know that when they find out that you're not at home, this will be the first place they will come looking."

"Don't worry Lily. I'll be leaving for Scotland on the ten o'clock train. I'm planning on staying with my aunt up in Aberdeen."

Lily Ann had insisted that Josie should have something to eat before leaving for the station.

While she was making something for Josie to munch on Drake, her younger brother, walked into the kitchen to get a glass of milk.

Lily Ann was startled.

"What are you doing up so early?"
"Wow sis, why are you shouting? I'm sorry if I scared you."

He paused for a split second as he looked at his sister suspiciously.

"Why are you up so early? We all know you're not an early morning person; and why are you unusually jumpy?"
Lily Ann barked at her brother.
"Keep quiet, and go back to bed."
"Okay, okay. Keep your hair on, I'm going, but you're definitely not yourself this morning."

As Drake backed out of the kitchen, he almost bumped into Josie.

"What are you doing here? I don't remember seeing you before I went to bed last night."
Lily pushed her brother out of the kitchen.
"Stop being nosey, and go to your room."

Josie looked worried.

"Lily, are you okay?"
"Yes, I'm okay. I don't know why I snapped. He just caught me

off guard."

"I hope I haven't gotten you into any trouble, especially now that Drake has seen me here. What if he calls Lois or Daphne, and tells them that he saw me? You know how your brother and my sisters chat for hours over the phone!"

"Don't worry about Drake, I'll handle him. I'm more concerned about you. I really hope you know what you're doing."

Josie could see the concern in her friend's eyes.

"It's okay Lily. I will keep in touch, and let you know how it's all going up in Scotland.

Come to think of it, I'm not really feeling that hungry anyway. Maybe I should just have a cup of coffee. I don't want to be here when your parents wake up, especially your mum!"

Lily agreed.

"Alright. Let me just put my coat on, and grab my purse."

Lily Ann and Josie left the house just a few minutes before six thirty in the morning.

They got on the bus and made their way to London St Pancras Station.

As the bus weaved through the traffic, both girls were quiet, deep in their own thoughts, maybe contemplating the upheaval that their action would cause once Josie's disappearance was discovered.

Finally, they jumped off at the station bus stop.

Lily Ann waited as Josie bought a one-way ticket to Aberdeen, then escorted her to the platform where the North East Coastal train was standing.

They both boarded the train, and Lily Ann helped her friend find a nice, journey facing seat.

Then she turned to Josie.

Josie had a forlorn, and vulnerable look in her eyes.

It was a sad sight, and Lily Ann found herself looking away when she felt the tears in her eyes.

As the departure time approached, they embraced each other. Then Lily Ann got off the train and stood on the platform.

The station guard blew his whistle, and the train slowly pulled away.

Both friends could hardly bare to look at each other as they waved goodbye.

At exactly ten o'clock on the last day of July, Josie started her journey to Aberdeen; a journey into the unknown.

I hope all you book lovers have enjoyed reading
this heart touching story.

Wondering what happens to Josie
when she gets to Aberdeen?
Will she ever get to see her daughter again?
What becomes of Michael Doland?

Find out in the sequel,
"RESTORATION."
(Summer 2017)

www.ingramcontent.com/pod-product-compliance
Lightning Source LLC
Chambersburg PA
CBHW020131180626
46810CB00004B/1511